KILL

JOY

also by Holly Jackson

A Good Girl's Guide to Murder

Good Girl, Bad Blood

As Good as Dead

Five Survive

KILL JOY

HOLLY JACKSON

Delacorte Press

Text copyright © 2022 by Holly Jackson
Cover photograph copyright © 2023 by Vera Lair/Stocksy; blood image copyright © 2023 by LoveTheWind/Getty Images; other images used under license from Shutterstock.com
Interior art used by license from Shutterstock.com

GetUnderlined.com

Educators and librarians, for a variety of teaching tools, visit us at RHTeachersLibrarians.com

Library of Congress Cataloging-in-Publication Data is available upon request.
ISBN 978-0-593-42621-0 (trade pbk.) — ISBN 978-0-593-42623-4 (ebook)

The text of this book is set in 11-point Utopia Std.
Interior design by Michelle Crowe

Printed in the United States of America
10 9 8 7 6 5 4
First American Ed

Dedicated to Mary Celia Collis

1925–2020

KILL
JOY

Dear Celia Bourne, (AKA Pip Fitz-Amobi)

You are cordially invited to come dine with me to celebrate my 74th birthday. The whole family will be in attendance for the weekend, and I expect you to be here too. It will be a night to remember.

Where: At Remy Manor on Joy—my private island off the west coast of Scotland. Remember, the boat only leaves the mainland once a day at 12:00 p.m. sharp and the journey takes two hours.
(But actually just at Connor's house.)

When: This weekend (Next Saturday at 7:30 p.m.)

Yours sincerely,

Reginald Remy

(but actually it's from me, Connor)

Please open this invitation for additional information.

KILL JOY GAMES™

YOUR CHARACTER

For this murder mystery game you will be playing the role of:

Celia Bourne

You are the twenty-nine-year-old niece of Reginald Remy, the patriarch of the Remy family and owner of the Remy Hotels and Casinos empire in London. You are an orphan; your parents died when you were young and you have never been truly welcomed into the Remy family, despite them being your only living relatives. You are bitter about this and the fact that the incredibly wealthy Reginald Remy has never offered to help you out financially. You currently work in London, as a governess to a well-off family.

Costume Suggestions

Get ready to go back in time, to 1924, and dive into the Roaring Twenties. A drop-waist evening dress should do the trick. Accessorize with a headband and a feather boa.

OTHER CHARACTERS

1. Robert "Bobby" Remy

the elder son of Reginald Remy—will be played by:

Ant Lowe

2. Ralph Remy

the younger son of Reginald Remy—will be played by:

Zach Chen

3. Lizzie Remy

the wife of Ralph Remy—will be played by:

Lauren Gibson

4. Humphrey Todd

the butler at Remy Manor—will be played by:

Connor Reynolds

5. Dora Key

the cook at Remy Manor—will be played by: Cara Ward

Prepare yourself for an unforgettable night of murder and mystery.

KILL JOY GAMES™

one

A smear of red across her thumb pressed into the hollows and spirals of her skin. Pip studied it like a maze. It could be blood, if she squinted. It wasn't, but she could trick her eyes if she wanted to. It was Ruby Woo, the red lipstick her mom had insisted she wear to "complete the 1920s look." Pip kept forgetting about it and accidentally touching her mouth: another smudge there on her little finger. Bloodstains everywhere, standing out against her pale skin.

They pulled up outside the Reynoldses' house. Pip had always thought the house looked like a face, the windows staring down at her.

"We're here, pickle," her dad said needlessly from the front of the car. He turned to her, a wide smile on his face, creasing his black skin and the gray-flecked beard he was "trying out for summer," much to her mom's dismay. "Have fun. I'm sure it'll be a night to *die* for."

Pip groaned. How long had he been planning to say that? Zach, beside her, gave a polite laugh. Zach was her neighbor; the Chens lived four doors down from the Amobis, so Pip and Zach were always in and out of each other's cars, getting rides to and back together. Pip had her own car now, since she'd turned seventeen, but it was in the shop this weekend. Almost like her dad had planned it so they'd have to suffer through his terrible murder-based jokes.

"Any more?" Pip said, wrapping the black feather boa around her arms, making them look even whiter. She opened the door, pausing to roll her eyes at him.

"Oh, if looks could *kill*," her dad said with a little too much flair.

There was always one more. "OK, goodbye, Dad," she said, stepping out, Zach mirroring her on the other side, thanking Mr. Amobi for the lift.

"Have fun," Pip's dad called. "You both look dressed *to kill!*"

And another. Annoyingly, Pip couldn't help but laugh at that one.

"Oh, and, Pip," her dad said, dropping the act, "Cara's dad is giving you a lift back. If you get home before Mom and I are back from the movie, will you let the dog out?"

"Yes, yes." She waved him off, walking up to the front door side by side with Zach. He looked slightly ridiculous, in a red blazer with navy stripes, crisp white pants, and a black bow tie, with a straw boater hat covering his straight dark hair. His little name badge read *Ralph Remy*.

"Ready, Ralph?" she asked, pressing the doorbell. And then again. She was impatient to get this over and done with. Sure, she hadn't seen her friends all together in weeks, and maybe this would be *fun*. But she had work waiting for her at home, and fun, after all, was just a waste of time. Still, she could pretend well enough, and pretending wasn't lying.

"After you, Celia Bourne." Zach smiled, and she could tell he was excited. Maybe she'd have to pretend a little better, arranging a grin on her face too.

It was Connor who opened the door, except he didn't exactly look like Connor Reynolds anymore. He'd put some kind of colored wax in his normally dark blond hair. It was now gray, and pasted neatly back from his face. There were brown wiggly face-paint lines around his eyes: a poor attempt at wrinkles. He was wearing a black tuxedo— it had to have been borrowed from his dad—and a matching white waistcoat and bow tie, with a napkin folded over one arm.

"Good evening." Connor bowed low, some of his gray hair unsticking and flopping forward with him. "Welcome back to Remy Manor. I'm the butler, Humphrey Todd," he said, emphasis on the "hump."

There was a squeal as Lauren appeared in the hallway behind Connor. She was wearing a red flapper dress, the tassels on the hem skimming her knees. A bell-shaped hat hid most of her ginger hair, and there was a string of pearls wrapped around her neck, knocking against her *Lizzie Remy* badge. "Is that my husband?" she said excitedly, bounding forward and dragging poor Zach into the house after her.

"I see everyone's already far too excited," Pip said, following Connor down the hall.

"Ah, well, it's good you've arrived to bring us all back down," he teased her.

She widened her grin and pretended even harder.

"Your parents home?" she asked.

"No, they're away for the weekend. And Jamie's out. House to ourselves."

Connor's brother, Jamie, was six years older than them, but he'd been living at home ever since he dropped out of college. Pip remembered back when it happened, how thick the tension had been in the Reynoldses' house, how they'd all learned to tiptoe around it. Now it was one of those not-talked-about topics.

They arrived in the kitchen, where Lauren had towed Zach and was now handing him a drink. Cara and Ant were there too, with matching glasses of red wine. An improvement on whatever concoctions they usually made from half-full bottles in unguarded drinks cabinets.

"'Ello, Madam Pip," Cara—Pip's best friend—said in a terrible cockney accent, sidling forward to fiddle with

Pip's feather boa before letting it flop back against her garish emerald-green dress. Pip missed her normal overalls. "How fancy."

"Thrift store," Pip replied, taking in Cara's costume. She was wearing a frumpy black dress with a long white cook's apron, her dark blond hair covered by a gray bandanna. She had also gone for the face-paint-wrinkle look, slightly more subtle and effective than Connor's. "How old is your character supposed to be?" Pip asked.

"Oh, ancient," Cara said. "Fifty-six."

"You look eighty-six."

Ant snorted, and Pip turned to him finally. He might have looked the most outlandish of them all, dressed in a pin-striped suit that was far too baggy on his small frame, a glossy white tie, a black bowler hat, and a giant fake mustache stuck to his upper lip.

"To freedom and summer," Ant said, holding up his wine for a moment before he took a sip. The mustache dipped into the liquid, droplets clinging to it as he re-emerged from the glass.

The "freedom" Ant meant was that they had all now finished their SATs; it was the end of June and the first time they'd all hung out like this—all six of them—in a while, despite living in the same town and attending the same school.

"Well, yes," said Pip, "except it's not really summer, because we still have a month left of school. "Plus there's college applications coming up, and we have to pick our topics for the senior capstone project soon." OK, maybe she needed a little more practice *pretending*. She couldn't help it; there'd been a twang of guilt in her chest as she left the house, reminding her that she really should have started work on that project today, even though she'd had her last exam only yesterday. Work breaks didn't sit well with Pip Fitz-Amobi, and "freedom" didn't feel very freeing.

"Oh my god, do you ever take a night off?" Lauren said, her eyes and thumbs down on her phone.

Ant jumped in. "We can give you some homework if that will make you feel better."

"You've probably already picked your topic anyway," Cara said, forgetting her accent.

"I haven't," Pip said. And that was the problem.

"Fuck," Ant said in mock horror. "Are you OK? Do you need us to call an ambulance?"

Pip stuck her middle finger up at him and used it to flick his fluffy fake mustache.

"No one touches the mustache," he said, backing away. "It's sacred. And I'm scared you'll pull out the real mustache underneath."

"As if you could grow a real mustache." Lauren snorted, eyes still down on her phone. She and Ant had had a very short-lived, doomed romance last year, which had amounted to approximately four drunken kisses. Now they were lucky if they could pry Lauren away from her current

6

boyfriend, Tom, who was no doubt on the other end of that phone screen.

"Right, ladies and gentlemen." Connor cleared his throat, grabbing another bottle of wine, and a Coke for Pip. "If you would all care to follow me into the dining room."

"Even me, the 'umble cook?" Cara said.

"Even you." Connor smiled, leading them across the hall toward the dining room at the back of the house. It was still there, that chip in the doorframe from when Connor had been skateboarding inside when they were twelve. Pip had told him not to at the time, but did anyone ever listen to her?

As Connor opened the door, the muffled squealing sounds from within became jazz music coming from the Alexa in the corner of the room. The dining table had been extended and covered with a white cloth crisscrossed with fold lines, and three long, thin candles flickered in the middle, dribbling red wax down their sides.

The places had already been set: plates, wineglasses, silverware, and linens all laid out, and a little place card on each plate. Pip's eyes sought out *Celia Bourne*. She found her seat, between Dora Key—Cara—and Humphrey Todd—Connor, directly opposite Ant.

"What's for dinner?" Zach said, holding his empty plate as he took his seat on the other side of the table.

"Oh yes," Cara barged in. "What 'av I—the cook—made for dinner, butler dear?"

Connor grinned. "I think tonight you probably ordered Domino's after you realized that making dinner for this many people on top of hosting a murder mystery party was too much effort."

"Ah, takeout pizza, my signature dish," Cara said, rearranging her heavy dress so she could take her seat.

Pip settled down as well, her eyes falling to the small booklet to the right of her plate, which was printed with the title *Kill Joy Games—Murder at Remy Manor*. It had her game name on it too: *Celia Bourne*.

"No one touch their booklets yet," Connor said, and Pip hastily withdrew her hand, rebuffed.

Connor stood in front of the wide windows. It was still light outside, although there was a strange pink-gray glow as heavy clouds rolled in to claim the evening. The wind was picking up too, making the trees at the end of the yard dance, howling between the gaps in the music.

"Right, first things first," Connor announced, holding out a Tupperware box. "Hand over your phones."

"Wait, what?!" Lauren looked disgusted.

"Yeah," Connor said, shaking the box at Zach, who handed his phone over without a glance. "It's 1924—we wouldn't have phones. And I want us all to concentrate on the game."

Ant dropped his in. "Yeah," he said, "because you'd just spend the whole time texting your boyfriend."

"I would not!" Lauren protested, sullenly placing her phone in the box too.

The rest of them were quiet; they'd all been thinking the same. And in that silence Pip swore she heard something upstairs. Like the shuffle of footsteps. But no, it couldn't be. They were home alone, Connor had said. She must have imagined it. Or maybe it was just the rattle of the wind.

Pip collected her and Cara's phones and placed them in the plastic box.

"Thank you," Connor said with a butler-esque bow. He took the Tupperware over to the sideboard at the back of the room and made a great show of placing the box inside a drawer, and then locking it with a small key. He then took the key and placed it on top of the radiator. Pip caught Lauren eyeing it.

"Right, so from now on, everyone has to stay in character," Connor said, directing his words at a sniggering Ant.

"Yep, it's me, Bobby," Ant said. And then, wrapping his arm around Zach's shoulder, he added: "Me and my bro."

Pip surveyed them. So those were Celia Bourne's cousins: Ralph and Bobby Remy. Ugh, spoiled brats.

"Very good, sir," Connor responded. "But isn't it peculiar that we are all gathered for a meal to celebrate Reginald Remy's seventy-fourth birthday and he hasn't turned up for dinner?" He paused and looked at them all pointedly.

"Yes, um, very peculiar," Cara said.

"Very unlike my uncle," added Pip.

Zach nodded. "Father is never late."

Connor smiled, pleased with himself. "Well, he must be somewhere in the manor; we ought to go and look for him."

They all watched him closely.

"I said we ought to go and look for him," Connor repeated.

"Oh, like *actually* go look for him?" Lauren asked.

"Yes, he must be somewhere. Let's split up and search."

Pip jumped to her feet and filed out of the room with the others. Well, Reginald Remy had obviously just been murdered; it was a murder mystery game, after all. But what were they looking for exactly? A picture of the dead man or something?

They passed a closet in the hallway that had a piece of paper stuck to it, with the words *Billiard Room* written on it.

Zach pulled the closet doors open and peered inside. "He's not in the billiard room," he said. "And neither is a billiard table, for that matter."

Cara and Ant started tussling, racing to be the first to reach the living room door, which had been labeled *The Library*. But Pip's feet pulled her the other way, toward the stairs, Zach right on her heels. If she *had* actually heard something, it must have come from above the dining room. But what was it? They were home alone.

They climbed up, but at the top they broke apart, Zach heading off hesitantly toward Connor's bedroom and Pip the other way, to the room that sat directly above the dining room. She knew that this room was Connor's dad's office, but the door told her that tonight it was *Reginald Remy's Study.*

The door creaked as she pushed it open. It was dark in here, the blinds shutting out the last of the evening light. Her eyes adjusted to a room full of half-formed shadows. She'd never been inside this room before and she felt a prickle of unease up her neck; was she even allowed in here?

Pip could see the dark, hulking form of the desk against the far wall, and what must have been a swivel chair. But something wasn't right. The chair was facing the wrong way, pointing toward her. And there was a shadow disrupting its clean outline. There was something in that chair. Or someone.

Pip felt her heart kick up in her chest as her fingers scaled the wall, searching for the light switch. She found it and flicked it, holding her breath.

The yellow light blinked on, filling in the shadows. Pip was right: there was someone slumped in that chair. And then her heart dropped, soured in her gut, and all she could see was the blood.

So much blood.

two

It was Jamie, Connor's older brother.

He wasn't moving.

His eyes were closed, his head sagged at a strange angle against his shoulder. And the entire front of his once-white shirt was soaked with blood, glistening in the new light, angry and red.

Her mind stalled, emptied out, and refilled itself with all that blood.

"J-Ja—" Pip began, but the word cut off, crashing against her gritted teeth as she watched Jamie. Wait . . . maybe he *was* moving. It looked like he was shaking, his chest shuddering.

Pip took a step forward. It wasn't her eyes tricking her; he really was shaking, she was sure of it. Shaking or juddering or . . .

. . . laughing. He was laughing, trying to hold it in, eyes opening and flicking up to her.

"Jamie," she said, annoyed. At him and at herself, really; of course it was just part of the game. She should have known right away.

"I'm sorry, Pip," Jamie chuckled. "Looks good, doesn't it? I look super dead."

"Yeah, super dead," she said, taking a deep breath to release the tightness in her chest. And now that she was closer, the fake blood was just a little *too* red, like the lipstick stains on her hands.

"I suppose you're Reginald Remy, then," she said.

"Sorry, can't answer you. I'm too dead," Jamie replied, rearranging the bright purple dressing gown he was wearing over the shirt. "Oh shit, everyone's coming." He dropped his head back and closed his eyes as Pip heard the others thundering up the stairs.

"Celia, where are you?" Cara called in her cockney accent.

"In here!" Pip shouted.

Zach was the first one to reach her from across the landing. He smiled when he peered in and saw Jamie. "Thought it was real for a sec," he said.

Lauren gasped as the others piled in behind her. "That's disgusting," she said. "And you said we were home alone, Connor."

"Golly," cried Connor. "It seems that Reginald Remy has been murdered!"

"Yeah, we got that part. Thanks, Connor," said Cara.

"That's *Humphrey* to you," he retorted.

There was a moment of silence as they looked expectantly at Connor. And then the dead body cleared his throat.

"What?" Connor turned to his brother.

"Your line, Con," said the corpse, moving as little as possible.

"Oh right. Everyone back to the dining room now," Connor announced. "I will call Scotland Yard at once . . . oh, and also order the pizza."

They were sitting back in their assigned places, Pip resisting the urge to peek at her booklet. A few minutes passed before Jamie strolled into the room. Except he wasn't the murdered Reginald Remy anymore. He had changed out of the bloody shirt into a clean black one. And on his head was a plastic police hat. He and Connor were very similar, even for brothers: freckled and blond. Though Connor was skinnier and more angular, and Jamie's hair a touch closer to brown. Jamie had offered to host the murder mystery so Connor could play along too.

"'Ello, 'ello, 'ello," Jamie said, standing at the head of the table, scrutinizing them all, a thicker Kill Joy Games booklet clutched in his hands. "I am Inspector Howard Whey, with the Scotland Yard police force. I understand that there has been a murder."

"Sal Singh did it!" Ant shouted suddenly, looking around, expecting a laugh.

The table went quiet.

Of course, there had been a murder—a real murder—in their town, Fairview, just over five years ago. Andie Bell, who had been the same age Pip was now, was murdered by her boyfriend, Sal Singh, who killed himself days later. An open-and-shut case of murder-suicide as far as the police were concerned. And everywhere in Fairview was a reminder of what happened: their school that Andie and Sal had both attended, the woods outside Pip's house where Sal was found, the bench dedicated to Andie on the town common, sightings of the Bells and the Singhs, who still lived here.

It was almost like Fairview itself was defined by the murder of Andie Bell, both names usually uttered in the same breath, inextricable from the other. Pip sometimes forgot how un-normal it was to have such a terrible thing so close to their lives, some closer than others. Cara's older sister, Naomi, had been best friends with Sal. That was how Pip had known him, and he'd always been so kind to her. She didn't want to believe it. But, as they said, open and shut. He did it. So he must have.

Pip looked up at Jamie and saw a flash of shock in his eyes. Jamie had been in that same school year, took the same classes as Andie.

15

"Shut up, Ant," Cara said seriously, no trace of the cook Dora Key.

"Yes," Jamie said, recovering. "Typical Bobby Remy, always interrupting and seeking attention. As I was saying"—he breezed past the awkwardness—"there has been a murder. Reginald Remy is dead, and because you are the only people on the secluded private island of Joy and there is only one boat a day, one of you must be the murderer!"

Their eyes shifted suspiciously to one another, and Pip noticed Cara avoiding Ant's gaze.

"But together we can solve this mystery and bring the killer to justice," Jamie continued, reading a line from his booklet. "Here," he said, holding up a Target bag, "I'm going to give you each a little notebook and a pen so you can keep a record of clues and theories." Jamie asked Connor to hand them around, and—as Humphrey Todd, the butler—he dutifully accepted.

Pip wasted no time writing her name on the first page of her notebook and started taking notes. Not that she cared—it was just a game—but she hated the sight of an underused notebook.

"To begin, how about we go around the table and introduce ourselves?" Jamie said. "I'm sure you are all well acquainted, but I would like to know a little more about our suspects. Let's start with you, Bobby," he said, nodding to Ant.

"Yep, OK." Ant stood up. "Hi, everyone. My name is Robert 'Bobby' Remy. I'm thirty-nine years old and I am the older, and *favorite*"—he said with a teasing glance at Zach—"son of Reginald Remy. I used to work for the Remy Hotels and Casinos empire and was due to inherit the company from my father, but a few years ago, I realized that hard work isn't really my thing and since then I've just been taking it easy in London. Thank god my father still pays me an allowance. Paid, I mean. Oh, my poor father, who could have done this?" He clutched his chest in an over-the-top manner.

"OK, next," Jamie said, pointing to Zach.

"Hi all," he said, standing, with an awkward nod around the table. "I'm Ralph Remy, Reginald's younger son, age thirty-six. I work for Remy Hotels and Casinos, and for the last few years my father had been training me to take over the company. He'd been retired for some time but still made most of the executive decisions. We worked well as a team. Um . . . oh," he said, pointing to Lauren, sitting two places over. "This is my lovely wife, Lizzie. We've been married four years and are very happy together." He went to pat Lauren awkwardly on the shoulder and then retook his seat.

"Me?" Lauren went next, getting to her feet. "I'm Lizzie Remy, née Tasker, thirty-two years old. I'm Reginald's daughter-in-law, married to Ralph. Yes, very happy, dear." She smiled down at Zach. "I also work at the family company and have been managing the flagship London casino. Some of you might not think I belong in this family, but I've earned my place here, and that's all I have to say."

"OK," Pip said, rearranging her feather boa as she stood. She felt slightly ridiculous, but she was here; she might as well try to enjoy it. And maybe she'd forget about the senior capstone project proposal waiting for her at home. Damn, now she'd thought about it again. "I'm Celia Bourne, age twenty-nine. Reginald Remy was my uncle. My parents both died tragically when I was younger, so the Remys are the only family I have. Though they probably need reminding of that," she said with a sharp look at Ant and Zach's side of the table. "How nice that you all work at the *family* company; I've never been offered such a thing. I'm currently working as a governess in London, teaching the children of a very welcoming family."

"Ooh, my detective skills are picking up on some tension here," Jamie said, tapping his police hat. "And the household staff?" He turned to Cara and Connor.

"Yes, I'm Humphrey Todd," Connor announced, rising from his chair. "Sixty-two years young. I've been working as the butler here at Remy Manor for the last twenty years. It hasn't always been easy living somewhere so remote. I have a daughter, you see, who I don't often get to visit. But Mr. Remy has always paid me fairly, and I have always had the utmost respect for my master. In that time, seeing each other every day, I believe we came to be good friends."

Ant snorted. "No one makes friends with the *staff*," he said.

"Bobby"—Zach turned to him, shocked—"don't be cruel."

"Very good, sir," Connor said, a bow of contrition in Ant's direction as he sat back down.

"Last but not least," Cara said about herself as she stood, the accent making a comeback. "I'm Dora Key. And I'm only fifty-six, even though I've heard some of you gossiping that I look eighty-six." A meaningful look down at Pip. "I'm the household cook. I haven't actually been at Remy Manor very long; I was hired about six months ago. There used to be more staff here, apparently, but after the master's wife died he started letting people go, but I guess he realized he couldn't survive without a cook. Me and old Hump here, we keep the place running, even if it is hard work."

"Excellent," Jamie said. "Now that we've got the introductions out of the way, let me tell you the details of the case so far from my initial inspection." He started reading aloud. " 'All of the guests arrived yesterday, Friday, on the same boat from the mainland, to stay for the weekend. This evening, on his birthday, Reginald Remy, aged seventy-four, was killed in his study from a fatal stab wound straight to the heart. He would have died instantly. There are no defensive wounds on the body, which meant that Reginald knew and trusted his killer, and they were able to get close to him without raising suspicion.' "

Pip scribbled away, already on her second page.

"Our next task, then, is to establish the time of death and your alibis. So if you would all like to turn to the first page in your booklets. No further."

Pip picked hers up and spread it open on her plate. She read the first page quickly, and then again, checking that Connor and Cara weren't looking her way, rearranging her face to guard Celia's secrets.

YOUR ALIBI

When asked where you were at the time of the murder, you claim that you were in bed, taking a nap. Your allergies had been playing up and you thought it best to try to get some rest before the big birthday dinner.

In this round:

- Listen carefully to the alibis of the other guests.
- When Lizzie Remy gives her alibi, you must cast doubt on it. Tell her it is very strange she says she was having a bath at that time, as the pipes are usually very loud right by your room when someone upstairs lets out the bathwater, and you did not hear that sound this evening.

three

"First order of business, then," Jamie said, settling into the chair at the head of the table, "is to work out when Reginald was last seen alive and by whom."

"Oh, I believe that was me. Me, Ralph," Zach said, nodding at his booklet and then glancing up, running his finger over the relevant paragraph. "Lizzie, Celia, and I"—he glanced in turn at Lauren and Pip—"were taking tea in the library with my father. The cook"—a nod to Cara—"brought us some scones and cake to have with it. The women left first, and when we were done, I walked my father to the grand staircase. He told me he was going to his study to get some things in order before the birthday meal. That was at around five-fifteen p.m."

"Did anyone see Reginald Remy after that time?" Jamie asked the room, tipping his police hat.

There were a few murmurs of "no," shaking heads, and shifting glances.

"All right, fifteen minutes past five," Jamie announced, and Pip copied the time down. "And then Pip—sorry"— Jamie squinted at her name badge—"Celia found the body at approximately six-thirty p.m. In game time, not real time," he said, noticing Pip's creased brow. "Great, we have our time window in which the murder was committed: between five-fifteen and six-thirty. So"—he paused, staring at each of them in turn—"where were all of you in that crucial one hour and fifteen minutes?"

Connor was the first to respond, as Humphrey Todd, the butler. "Well, I was in here, setting up the dining room for the meal. The master always liked the silverware to be polished for special occasions."

"Have you got any proof?" Ant asked with all the pomposity of his part, Bobby Remy.

"My proof is the very table you are sitting at, young sir," Connor said, looking affronted. "When else do you think I would have had time to prepare this room?"

"And where were you, Bobby?" Zach asked his in-game brother. "You didn't take tea with us in the library like you were supposed to. In fact, you've been missing all after- noon."

"All right, you narc," Ant said. "If you must know, I went on a walk for a bit of soul-searching. By the cliffs. I'm sure, Ralph"—he returned the brotherly glare to Zach—"you understand why."

"But I went for a walk of the grounds too," Zach said.

"After I said goodbye to Father, I went for a stroll around the south side of the island, to burn off the scones and work up my appetite for dinner."

"Oh really?" Cara said as Dora Key, the cook, settling her elbows on the table. "That's interesting, because I was there too, and I didn't see you, Ralph. I can't be sure exactly where I was at the time, Inspector"—she glanced at Jamie—"as the clock in the kitchen has been broken for some time. But I'm pretty sure it was then that I walked to the vegetable patch on the south side of the grounds. And I don't remember seeing anyone else."

"Our paths must not have crossed," Zach said to her across the table.

"Clearly," Cara said. "And what about you, Pip—crap—Celia. Were you *also* taking a stroll on the grounds?"

Pip cleared her throat. "No, I wish. In fact, my allergies have been playing up since I arrived on the island, and I wanted to be on good form for tonight. So after tea in the library, I actually put myself to bed to get some rest before dinner."

"Where?" Ant asked.

"In my bedroom, of course," she replied hastily, surprising herself. Was she feeling defensive? Celia wasn't even a real person—why was she defending her? Too much attention was being paid to her; she should deflect. "You're being very quiet, Lizzie—where were you?"

"Oh," Lauren smiled sweetly. "Well, at tea I somehow managed to get jam all over me, so I decided to have a bath to spruce up before dinner. So that's where I was, in the tub in my room. Have you heard of bathing, Celia dear?"

"For an hour and fifteen minutes?" Pip countered.

"I take long baths."

"Hmm, that's interesting, though." Pip pulled a face. "The pipes to upstairs run right by my room, and I can always hear when someone lets out their bathwater; makes a right racket." She paused for effect, looked at the others. "The pipes were silent this evening."

Cara performed a dramatic gasp.

"I thought you said you were asleep." Lauren looked flustered. "How could you have heard anything anyway?"

Pip didn't have an answer for that.

"OK, that's very interesting," Jamie said now, scratching his chin. "It seems that each of you was alone at the time of the murder. Which, in fact, means that none of you, not one of you, has an alibi."

Cara supplied another gasp, but she put far too much into it and started to cough. Pip patted her on the back.

"So," Jamie continued, "you all . . . Wait, Connor, you ordered the pizza, right?"

"Yes, yes," Connor said.

"Good, just checking," he said, before slipping into the ultra-serious Inspector Howard Whey again. "So every

25

single one of you had means and opportunity to commit this murder. I wonder who among you also had a motive."

His gaze landed on Pip for a moment, and she shifted awkwardly beneath it. She didn't know much about Celia at this point; it was possible she actually was the murderer.

"But there is one last thing I found on my initial search of the study: the murder weapon." Jamie placed his knuckles on the table and leaned into them. "It was left beside the body; no fingerprints, so our killer must have worn gloves or wiped it afterward. It was a knife—one of the kitchen knives."

Everyone turned to look at Cara.

"What?!" she said, crossing her arms. "Oh, I see, blame it all on the poor cook, eh? Any one of you could have come into the kitchen and taken one of the knives."

"Not if you were in there," Zach said quietly, dropping his eyes. Confrontation wasn't really his thing, even when he wasn't being Zach.

"I wasn't," she protested. "I told you, I went to the vegetable patch. Look, come with me." She stood up. "Come with me, I said. I have proof."

She stormed out of the dining room.

"I guess we should follow her," Jamie said, beckoning to the rest of them.

This must have been part of the game, something

written in Cara's booklet. Pip's chair scraped the floor as she stood up and hurried out of the room, her notebook and pen in hand, following Cara into the kitchen.

"Aha," Ant said as he entered, pointing to the Reynoldses' cylindrical knife rack, the knives color-coded at the base of each handle. "Even more knives. How many more murders are you planning, Dora?"

"Well, those are far too modern for 1924," Pip said.

"If you'd all stop chitchatting," Cara said, "somewhere in here is a note that one of the guests left me. That's my proof. Help me find it."

"You mean this?" Connor said, fishing out an envelope from between two plates on the drying rack. Printed on the top side were the words *Clue #1.*

"Yes, that," Cara said, a small smile creeping on to her face. "Read it out loud to everyone."

Darlene,

For dinner tonight I am requesting a carrot cake to be made for dessert. It is the birthday boy's favorite, after all. Make sure it's moist.

—RR

Kill Joy Games™

Cara shuddered. "Urgh, I hate the word *moist*."

"Who's Darlene?" Connor asked, screwing his eyes up at the note.

"Well, clearly someone can't be bothered to learn my actual name," Cara said. "So I had to go to the vegetable patch to get the carrots. I made the bloody carrot cake, by the way. It was *moist* as fuck."

"It's signed off by RR," Pip thought aloud, turning to Ant and Zach: Robert and Ralph Remy. "One of you must have written it."

There was a blank expression on Zach's face, but Ant smiled and held up his hands. "OK, OK," he said. "I wrote that note. I was actually trying to do something nice for my father."

"For once," Zach quipped, getting into it now.

"I admit, my father and I haven't been as close recently. It was just meant as a nice gesture after we had a slightly fraught conversation this morning. But someone went and killed him before he ever got to see the damn carrot cake."

"What time did you leave this note, Bobby?" Pip asked, studying his eyes, her pen poised. Well, she didn't want to miss any important details, did she? OK, it was *just* a game, but even so, Pip didn't like to lose.

"It was late morning, I think," Ant replied, checking the detail in his booklet. "Yep, elevenish. The cook wasn't in here."

"See, told you," Cara said defiantly.

Pip turned to her. "I'm not sure this is an 'I told you so' moment."

Cara's look of triumph hardened into one of betrayal. "'Ow's that?" she asked, Dora Key's voice back in full force.

"Bobby left this note for you at eleven," Pip explained. "You could have gone to the vegetable patch at any time after that. This doesn't prove that that's where you were at the exact time of the murder."

"Are you calling me a liar?" Cara said, giving Pip a playful shove.

"In addition," Pip carried on, "this shows that at some point during the day you left the kitchen unattended, which means any one of us could have come in to take the knife." *Even me,* she thought. Well, Celia. "We know that Bobby was in here alone when he left the note. This note could even be his cover for having access to the murder weapon and—"

But her spiel was cut short by a loud, tinny noise that screamed through the house.

Another scream joined it.

four

"It's just the doorbell," Jamie said, eyeing a shrieking Lauren. She stopped immediately, trying—and failing—to disguise it as a cough. "Pizza's here!" Jamie hurried off to answer the front door, remembering only at the very last second to remove his plastic police hat. At least he wasn't covered in blood anymore.

"Texas BBQ, anyone?" Connor said a few minutes later, passing a pizza box to Zach across the dining table.

"I'm a frickin' great chef," Cara said, a line of stringy cheese clinging to her chin.

There were three slices on Pip's plate, but she hadn't touched them yet. She was hunched over her small notebook, writing down everyone's alibis and her initial theories. So far, things weren't looking great for Bobby, she thought with a secret glance across at Ant. But was that just what the game wanted her to think? Or was it simply because Ant was annoying even at the best of times? She needed to think objectively, remove herself and her feelings from the equation.

"OK," Jamie said, taking a break from his pizza, the hat now sitting at a jaunty angle on his head. "I'm glad to see that none of your appetites have been affected by this ghastly murder. But while you've been eating, I have completed my second inspection of the crime scene and have uncovered something very interesting indeed."

"What is it?" Pip demanded, her pen hovering above the page. Maybe she'd been wrong before. Maybe solving murders wasn't too different from homework after all. She could feel herself falling headfirst into it, the rest of the world fading out, like when she got lost in one of her essays or listening to an entire true crime podcast series in one night, or anything, really. Teachers called it "excellent focus," but Pip's mom worried that it fell much closer to obsession.

"Oh boy, the demon has awoken," Cara said with a playful prod between Pip's ribs. She'd been doing that since they were six years old, whenever Pip was *too* serious. "This is for fun, remember, Celia."

"I don't think the staff should touch members of the family," Lauren said, looking down her nose.

"Suck my dick, Lauren," Cara replied with a big gulp of wine.

"It's Lizzie."

"Oh, my apologies. Suck my dick, then, Lizzie."

"Right," Jamie laughed, raising his voice slightly. "On my second inspection I discovered that the safe hidden behind the family portrait in Reginald's study was left open. And . . . it's empty."

Cara performed another gasp and Jamie gave her a grateful nod.

"Exactly," he said. "Someone has broken into the safe and removed the contents. Ralph informed me that his father kept important documents in there."

"Did I?" Zach asked.

"Yes, you did," Jamie said. "This might have happened before or after the murder, but it certainly points to a possible motive." He cast his eyes back down to his master booklet. "But what secrets was Reginald keeping in there? Whatever was taken, by one of you, it's possible that the evidence is still somewhere in the house. Perhaps we should go and look for—"

Pip needed no further encouragement; she was the first up and out of the room this time, the others laughing at her. Where to? They'd been in the kitchen not long ago; the evidence was probably somewhere else. The library? That had come up in the story a few times already.

She headed toward the living room, *The Library* sign flapping against the door, straining against its tape. The wind must have found its way inside through some small, unknown crack. Behind her Pip heard Cara and Lauren bounding up the stairs. Were they heading to Reginald's study? It wouldn't be in there, whatever it was they were looking for; that was where it had been stolen from.

She stood at the threshold and surveyed the room. Large corner sofa and an armchair where they normally lived. The dark screen of the TV against the far wall, and she a faceless ghost reflected back in it, hanging strangely in the doorway. There was one shelf above the fireplace with two plants and eight books on it. Bit of a stretch to call it a library, but hey.

She stepped forward. On the arm of one of the sofas was a newspaper. She checked but it wasn't a clue; it was the Fairview town paper, open to an article about traffic-calming measures on Main Street, written by a Stanley Forbes. Riveting stuff.

Resting on top of the paper was a roll of tape. Jamie must have finished labeling the rooms in here.

Another ghost appeared in the TV and a floorboard creaked behind her, making her flinch. She whipped her head around, but it was only Zach.

"Found anything?" he asked, fiddling with his straw hat.

"Not yet," she said.

"Might be inside something, like a book." Zach crossed the room to the bookshelf above the fireplace. He pulled one out and flipped through it, shook his head and re-placed it.

Pip joined him, starting at the other end of the shelf. She pulled out a paperback copy of Stephen King's *It* and flicked through with her thumb. Something jumped out at her, gliding down to the floor.

"What is it?" Zach asked.

"Oh crap." Pip knelt to pick it up, realizing what it was. "It's nothing. It's a bookmark. Oops." She gritted her teeth and slotted the bookmark back in around page 400. It must have come from somewhere around there. Hopefully no one would notice, especially not Connor's dad, who was scary at the best of times.

She leaned one hand into the floor to push herself up and reshelve the book, but she stopped, eye-to-eye with the fireplace. There was something here. Scattered among the dark coals. Ripped-up pieces of white paper. And on that one there at the very top was the word *Clue.*

"Zach, I mean, Ralph, it's here," she said, gathering up the bits of paper and laying them out on the floor. "Some-one tried to destroy it."

"What is it?" He got to his knees, helping her pull the last of the shreds from the fireplace. Eighteen in all.

"I'm not sure yet, but there's writing on every piece. It looks typed. We need to stick it back together somehow. . . . Oh, hey, Zach, can you grab that tape from the sofa?"

He brought it back and, with his teeth, ripped off little squares of tape, sticking one edge to the floor. Lining them up, ready and waiting for her.

Pip went through the papers, catching fragments of words and reshuffling them into phrases and sentences. Arranging them until they fit, like a puzzle. Her eyes stalled on the repetition of the word *bequeath*. "It looks like it's Reginald's will or something," she said, adding another piece to complete the row of text as Zach gently applied tape along the cracks to stick them back together.

They heard a disturbance out in the hall. Scuffling and giggling. And then Ant's voice:

"Inspector, I need to report a very serious crime: the butler has stolen my mustache!"

"Done," Pip said, holding out the ripped-up document, shiny from the tape and slightly deformed in its resurrection. On one side it said *Clue #2* and on the other was printed *The Last Will and Testament of Reginald Remy*.

"We should go show the others," Zach said, straightening up.

Pip almost tripped on their way back to the dining room, unable to tear her eyes away from the page. Had the old bastard left anything to her?

"Found it?" Jamie asked them, finishing off his last pizza crust, and Pip held up the will in answer. The inspector called for the others to return to the dining room and take their seats. Ant was the last to file in, having managed to wrestle his mustache back from Connor, though it now sat wonkily on his face.

"Celia and Ralph have found something that must have been stolen from the safe," Jamie said. "Celia, if you could do us the honor and read it aloud."

THE LAST WILL AND TESTAMENT OF REGINALD REMY

I, Reginald Remy, being of sound mind, declare this to be my Last Will and Testament. I revoke all wills and codicils previously made by me.

To my son, Ralph Remy, I bequeath total ownership of my company, Remy Hotels and Casinos, to run as he sees fit. In addition, I leave to him Remy Manor on Joy island and the London townhouse and a sum of 2 million pounds.

To my daughter-in-law, Elizabeth Remy, I bequeath a sum of 500,000 pounds and my racehorse, Blue Thunder, as I know she has always loved going to the races.

To my niece, Celia Bourne, I bequeath a sum of 200,000 pounds, and the artwork painted by my late sister (her mother). I know that will mean a lot to her.

And finally, to the household staff, it is my wish that they will be paid their wage from my estate for a total of six months after my death, while they look for new employment.

Date: 17/08/1924

Reginald Remy

Jamie had appeared behind Pip, looking at the document over her shoulder.

"It looks like this will was drawn up recently, just last week," he pointed out.

But there was another glaring thing too. Pip had known even as she was trying to concentrate on reading it out, her eyes flicking away from her, searching out the gaps like they couldn't believe it either.

She looked up and studied their faces. Had any of them noticed? Ant hadn't; he was too busy fiddling with his mustache.

"Have you realized?" she asked the group, eyes circling them and coming to land on Ant.

"Realized what?" he asked.

"Robert 'Bobby' Remy," Pip said, offering Ant the document, "you've been written out of your father's will."

five

"Bullshit. Let me see that." Ant snatched the will out of Pip's outstretched hand. He ran his eyes down the page. "That fucker," he said, "he really left me nothing? I'm his oldest son. Even the staff get something."

"We found it in the fireplace," Pip explained to the others. "Someone tried to destroy it. It was ripped to shreds."

"Are you implying that that was me?" Ant said defensively, dropping the page onto his empty plate.

"Doesn't look great for you," said Zach.

"Why?" Ant replied.

The Remy brothers glared at each other, though Pip could see they were both close to smiling and breaking character, the situation not helped by Ant's crooked mustache.

"Because," Pip said, "your father wrote up a new will

last week, removing you from it. And today someone broke into the safe in your father's study and tried to destroy that document so that his old will would stand. Oh, and then your father was murdered. Desperate for some cash, are you?"

"It wasn't me," Ant said. "I didn't break into that safe and I didn't destroy that will."

"Mm-hmm," Cara added. "Sounds exactly like what a murderer would say."

"And didn't you say you had a 'fraught conversation' this morning?" Pip said, reading back through her scribbled notes. "Was it fraught because he told you he'd written you out of his will?"

"No." Ant fiddled with his collar. "We just always had fraught conversations."

"Well, this is all very interesting," Jamie said, glancing down at his master booklet. "And on the topic of fraught conversations, I wonder if anyone else has overheard anything this weekend? Anything that now, in light of the murder, seems suspicious or out of place. Please turn to page two in your booklets but no farther."

Pip bounded back to her chair, disentangling herself from her feather boa, and flipped to the next page.

In this round:

- Ralph Remy will tell a story about hearing a woman on the telephone last night saying some very strange things indeed. It was **you** he heard, and you must admit to it. However, you should tell the group that you were simply discussing your employment contract and your upcoming working dates with the family that employs you as a governess. Make them believe it.

- To counter, you must tell the group about a damning conversation you overheard between Ralph and his father on your way to said phone call. Walking past the study, you heard them talking in there, raising their voices. Some particular phrases you overheard Ralph say are: "I refuse to do that, Father," "This scheme of yours is ridiculous and will never work," and "won't get away with this."

Pip finished reading and looked up. From the corner of her eye she could see that Cara was watching her closely, a small smile creeping across her face. Pip clutched her open booklet against her dress so Cara couldn't see it, holding her secrets close to her chest. What did Cara know? Or was Pip just being paranoid, reading too much into it?

Make them believe it. That must mean it wasn't true. Why was Celia lying? What did she have to hide? Now Pip would have to lie and hide it too.

"Well"—Ant cleared his throat—"I did overhear a conversation between my father and the butler yesterday." Connor straightened in his chair. "Oh, nothing too bad." Ant smiled. "I just remember my father remarking to you that he was dreading his birthday. Of course, we all know why that is, considering what happened on this day last year."

The table was silent.

"I don't know what happened last year," Jamie said. "Someone care to enlighten me?"

"Well, Inspector . . ." Ant turned to him. "There was a tragic accident."

A sudden movement drew Pip's eyes away from Ant. Zach had just flinched in his chair, brushing one hand up his arm. Must have been a fly or something.

"The family were all staying at Remy Manor for my father's birthday," Ant continued. "In the afternoon, I took a walk of the grounds with my mother, Rose Remy. It was just a normal pleasant walk, a sunny day, perhaps a little windy. I don't really know how it happened—just a terrible, terrible accident."

Zach winced again, inadvertently kicking a table leg.

Pip narrowed her eyes and studied him across the table. Twice within thirty seconds, that was weird. She replayed Ant's words in her head. Wait, there was a pattern here. Both times Zach had flinched right after Ant said the word *accident*. Was he doing it intentionally or was she just too hyperaware, reading something out of nothing?

"I must have been walking ahead of her, because I didn't see it happen," Ant said. "But I heard her scream and turned back just as she fell off the cliff. We were so high up; the doctors said she died instantly on impact." He looked down and sighed. "I don't know if she stumbled or tripped or something. Just a terrible freak accident."

Pip was ready for it this time—her eyes peeled and fixed on Zach. He flinched, running his fingers awkwardly up his neck, catching her eye for less than a second. Yes, he was doing it on purpose; it had happened too many times now to be a coincidence. It must have been something his booklet told him to do, to physically react whenever his brother said the word *accident*. And what did that mean? Well, clearly, Ralph Remy didn't believe that his mother's death was an accident at all. Maybe he secretly thought Bobby had pushed her, that he had murdered her.

Pip grabbed her notebook, scribbling this all down in hasty bullet points.

"Father was never the same after her death," Ant said quietly.

"No." Zach patted him on the back. "The whole thing was so strange; she used to walk those cliffs every single day. She was always so careful, would never go near the edge."

"Indeed," Ant agreed, though Pip was sure now that Zach's words meant something very, very different. He thought his own brother had killed her. And now his father had been murdered too. Talk about a dysfunctional family. Maybe it was good they'd never welcomed her in.

"Tragic." Jamie nodded solemnly. "Tragedy striking twice on Reginald's birthday. Did anyone else hear anything strange or suspicious this weekend?"

Zach raised his hand. Here it came; he was about to turn on her. *Game face on, Pip.*

"Yes, I did," he said tentatively, reading from his booklet. "Last night—it was quite late—I heard a voice downstairs in the hall on the way to my bedroom. It was a woman's voice, and I think she was talking on the telephone. I listened for a little while. She was saying a whole stream of numbers, like *five, thirty-one, twelve, seven,* on and on in some nonsensical stream. Very bizarre." He paused. "And then she was talking low, whispering, and I couldn't really pick anything up, other than hearing her repeat the word *terminate*." He glanced nervously at Pip. "It wasn't Lizzie's voice, and I doubt it was the cook...."

"If you're going to accuse me of something, you might as well say it with some conviction," Pip said with her sweetest, sharpest smile.

"OK, it was you, Celia," he said. "What were you doing? Who were you on the phone with?"

"You're going to feel very foolish," Pip said. "There was nothing suspicious going on at all. I was simply talking to my employer. You've never shown much interest, cousin, but as I stated earlier, I work as a governess, teaching the children of a well-to-do family. As is evident, I had to take some time off to be here for my uncle's birthday. So I was on the phone going through my employment contract and telling him when he could expect me back, you know, as I don't want him to *terminate* my contract. And as for those numbers, he simply wanted to know the upcoming dates for his eldest child's mathematics tests."

"Quite late to be having a phone call with your boss," Lauren commented, coming to her husband's aid.

"Well, being a governess is a twenty-four seven job, Lizzie," Pip said. "Not that you'd understand, living on cozy handouts from the family you married into."

"Oooooh, burn," Cara laughed, offering up a high five.

"But I'm glad you brought up the topic of suspicious conversation, Ralph," Pip said, resting her elbows on the table, her chin in the bed of her knuckles. "Because I actually overheard one of yours on my way to making said phone call."

"Aha, the plot thickens," Connor said, clumsily picking up his pen, though he didn't actually start writing.

"You were with your father in his study—the scene of his murder—having a very heated discussion."

"Is that right?" Zach said, crossing his arms.

"Oh yes. And I picked up a few specific phrases from the harsh words you were exchanging with your father." She glanced down at her booklet for accuracy. "At one time you told him, 'I refuse to do that, Father.' Then you said, 'This scheme of yours is ridiculous and will never work.' And then the last thing I heard you say before I walked away was: 'won't get away with this.' Care to elaborate on your argument with a man who was murdered less than twenty-four hours later?"

"Yes, I do care to elaborate," Zach said, attempting the sneer Ralph might have worn, but it kept turning up at the corners into a smile. "We were talking business, OK? We still worked closely together on matters relating to his hotel and casino empire, making decisions. The truth is that the business hasn't been doing so well of late, and we are under pressure from our main competitors in the luxury hotel and casino business, the Garza family."

Cara sniffed to Pip's left, distracting her. Or maybe it was another sound she'd heard. Like a thud or a muffled bang coming from outside. It was probably nothing, and Zach was speaking again. . . .

"As you know, the Garza family have long been our rivals, and it has gotten a lot less friendly and a lot more ugly since dear Mother died." Zach turned to the inspector to offer an explanation. "Our mother used to be friends—well, at least friendly—with the wife of Mr. Garza. But of late the Garzas have been very much stepping on our turf, so to speak, because we bring in more money than them . . . just. Father and I were having a disagreement about a business strategy to ensure people were still coming to our casino, not the Garzas'. That's all. We often had disagreements about the business, but it always worked out."

"And the 'won't get away with this'?" Pip asked.

"Well, that was a slightly different conversation," Zach admitted. "Father told me that he'd had someone check out the books, and it looked as though someone was skimming money from the London casino, one of the employees."

The non-Remy side of the table stared down the Remy side.

"Hey, don't look at ol' Bobby," Ant said. "Daddy fired me years ago. Can't be me."

"Someone stealing? At my casino?" Lauren asked.

"You mean the one you manage, Lizzie," said Pip.

Zach nodded. "So I just said we'd look into it and the thief won't get away with it or something. Nothing suspicious here either." He held up his hands.

That was when Pip heard it again. Or thought she heard it, something outside. She turned to the window. It was dark now, well on its way to pitch-black.

"What?" Cara asked her.

"I think I heard something outside," she said.

"What?" said Lauren, losing the haughty edge of Lizzie Remy.

"I'm not sure."

They listened, but the up-tempo jazz was too loud, the saxophone drowning everything else out.

"Alexa, pause music!" Connor called.

The music cut off and Pip listened. It was a loud kind of quiet; the breath of the others, the sound of her own tongue moving around her mouth, the whistling of the wind.

And then it happened again.

A crash outside in the darkening garden.

six

Connor's head snapped to his brother, panic pooling in the black of his eyes.

Jamie held them for a moment, before his face split with a smile. "God, you guys are jumpy," he said. "It's just the shed door; sometimes it bangs open in the wind. It's fine."

"Are you sure?" Lauren said. Her arm had somehow looped itself through Ant's, Pip noticed.

"Yes," Jamie laughed, and then added, "Youth today."

"Well, excuse us for growing up in murder town," Lauren countered, reclaiming her arm with an awkward glance at Ant.

"Could be ghosts," Ant said, his cheeks flushed. "I certainly know of two local vengeful spirits who could fit the bill."

"Ant . . . ," Cara said in a warning voice.

"Everything's fine," Jamie said. "Just ignore it. Alexa! Resume music and volume up. See, can hardly hear it anymore. No *actual* murder tonight, kiddos. Right, back to 1924." He straightened his hat and Pip picked up her pen again. "As any detective knows, a killer must have a motive. I wonder if anyone among us might have held a grudge against the late Reginald Remy. A reason to hate him. Please turn to your next page."

In this round:

- You must reveal a tense interaction you witnessed between Lizzie and Reginald Remy earlier this evening. When you were taking tea in the library with Lizzie, Ralph, and Reginald, Lizzie spilled some jam from her scone on her hand and her dress. Reginald commented to her that she often had "sticky fingers." Lizzie seemed shocked and soon left the room to go clean herself up.
- Pay close attention to the other secrets being revealed.

KILL JOY GAMES™

Pip looked up, her eyes trailing over to Lauren, watching her read her own booklet and biting her lip in concentration. And then Lauren's eyes flicked up, straight to her, and Pip's stomach dropped. They held each other's gaze for a long moment, until Lauren sniffed and broke it, her mouth downturned in a scowl.

Sticky fingers? That meant someone who steals, didn't it? A thief. Oh shit.

Pip grabbed her notebook and started to write, her fingers trying to keep up with her head. Reginald and Ralph had had a conversation last night about how someone was stealing from the London casino, the place Lizzie Remy managed. And today Reginald made a pointed remark to her about *sticky fingers.* He must have thought she was the one who was stealing! And judging by Lizzie's reaction, maybe Reginald was right on the money. And if Lizzie knew that Reginald knew . . . Well, that was certainly motive enough to kill him. Her only other choice would have been jail.

Pip's thoughts were interrupted by Zach clearing his throat and launching into a speech as Ralph. "Well, yes, Inspector, if you are talking about any ill feeling within the family, I'm afraid there was quite a lot between my brother, Bobby, and my father. As is no doubt evidenced by him being written out of the will."

Ant reacted by poking Zach in the face, a bit too close to his eye.

Zach recoiled. "Ow."

"Just a bit of brotherly love," Ant said, his words slightly slurred.

"Anyway," Zach continued, "this ill feeling really began several years ago, back when Bobby used to work for my father and was still heir to the casino empire. Being around casinos all day, Bobby developed a serious gambling addiction. He was always in debt and borrowing money. And when banks would no longer lend to him, he turned to a less reputable source. He borrowed money from a gang of loan sharks and then, of course, lost it all gambling again. And when he couldn't pay the gang back, they threatened to kill him. So my father bailed Bobby out, paid off the loan sharks and all his other debts to save his life. But from that day on my father forbade Bobby from working with or having anything to do with the Remy business again. He said he would continue to pay Bobby a monthly allowance to live comfortably, but if Bobby ever gambled again, even once, Father promised that he would cut him off for good. An ultimatum."

"Yes." Ant nodded. "That is all true. I borrowed money from the wrong people; it was a gang called the East End Streeters, if you must know. But I don't know why you think that means I had a grudge against our father. He saved me. And more than that, he continued to pay me to do nothing. Literally a perfect situation for me. No grudge here."

"Ah," Jamie the inspector said, reading from his script. "The East End Streeters are a nasty bunch. We at Scotland Yard have had a lot of dealings with them. They're in the cocaine business, you see. Among other illegal activities. Earlier this year my partner was working undercover to track their cocaine dealings, but they must have figured it out. They murdered him, shot him dead in the street. Very nasty business. I'm glad to see you came out the other side unharmed, Bobby."

"Thank you, Inspector."

Kiss-ass, Pip thought as she filled another page in her notebook.

"Does anyone else know someone here who bore ill will to Reginald?" Jamie asked.

Pip raised her hand. "Earlier this evening," she said, avoiding Lauren's eyes, "Lizzie, Ralph, and I were having tea and scones in the library with Reginald, as you've already heard. But there was a moment when Lizzie spilled jam on her hands and clothes and she was making a fuss; Reginald looked at her and made a comment about her often having 'sticky fingers.'" Pip paused. "You could have cut the tension in the room with a knife. Lizzie looked shocked and soon made excuses to leave the room."

"Oh, *sticky fingers,* eh, Lizzie?" Cara said, waggling her eyebrows.

"It means someone who steals," Pip clarified.

Cara deflated. "Oh, that's not as fun."

Lauren laughed, waving her hand dismissively. "That's nothing. There was no tension, and I'm not sure what you're implying." She stared Pip down. "Reginald loved to tease me, as his only daughter-in-law, and I'm very clumsy, always spilling food down myself, hence the *sticky fingers*."

"Sure, Jan," Cara said, her face re-creating that meme. "Anyway, I have something too."

The table turned its attention to her, and Dora Key the cook came out in full force, Cara sitting up as tall as she could, fiddling with her apron.

"As the only members of staff here, Humphrey and me often have conversations of an evening, after our work is done. To pass the time. And, well"—she side-glanced across Pip, aiming it at Connor—"this last week our conversations have taken a bit of a dark turn. Very disturbing in light of what's happened."

"What?" Pip said, impatient.

"Well, earlier this week, Humphrey was complaining about the master, and I said, 'Oh, he's not that bad.' To which Humphrey replied, 'I hate him.' Someone gasp, please."

Jamie and Zach enthusiastically granted her request. Pip was too busy writing.

"Yes, thank you." Cara nodded at them. "But that's not the worst part."

"It gets worse?" Ant said, staring at Connor. "Not looking so great for you, Humphrey. It's always the butler, eh?"

"Much worse," Cara said, looking dramatically at each of them in turn. "Just a couple of days ago, Humphrey was talking about Reginald Remy, and he turned to me, this terrible glint in his eyes, and he said, 'I wish he were dead.'"

seven

The room was silent, just the up-and-down notes of the muted trumpets while Connor squirmed in his chair.

"Thanks, Dora, for revealing our *private* conversations," Connor said, emphasizing the word.

"I had to tell the truth." Cara put up her hands. "A man is dead."

"Yes, but not because of me."

"Is it true?" Pip asked. "Did you say that? Did you wish Reginald dead?"

"Yes, I said it, but I didn't mean it." Connor fiddled with his white bow tie like it was tightening around his neck, trying to strangle him. "I was just blowing off steam. I'm sure most butlers have choice words about their masters. And, well, I was annoyed at him because a couple of weeks ago I asked him for some time off, and Reginald outright denied me. Said he was too busy to let me go at the moment with no notice, no matter how much I begged."

"Why did you want time off?" Pip asked, pen ready and waiting above the page.

"To visit my daughter. I hardly ever see her. And now it's . . . It was important to me, and I was angry, that's all. But that doesn't make me a murderer."

"Makes you look sketchy as fuck, though," Ant said.

"You can talk, Bobby," Pip countered.

"And anyway, if we are talking about *sketchy*"—Connor finally unclipped his tie, pointing a finger back at Cara—"let's talk about Dora Key, shall we? Since you decided to spill my secrets."

"Fine by me. I'm an open book, or an open *cook*," Cara said with a wink.

Pip was caught between the two; she pushed her chair back so she could watch the altercation.

"Oh really?" Connor steepled his fingers. "Well, how about this, then? Dora Key was hired by Reginald only six months ago. I knew the cook before her very well; we'd worked together for fifteen years. Then, all of a sudden, out of the blue, she quits, with no real reason. She'd never mentioned leaving to me before. And as she left, just before she got on the boat to the mainland, she told me that someone was forcing her to quit, threatening her life, but she couldn't say who. And then, two days later, Dora Key turns up. The new cook. And your food is terrible. So who are you and why are you really here?"

"How dare you? I made you Domino's Pizza," Cara said, trying to fight a smile. "Even extra pepperoni."

"OK, OK," Jamie stepped in, silencing them all. "It's clear that there are a lot of secrets in this room. And some of those secrets might be linked to the murder. But right now it's time for you to learn your own biggest secret. Please turn to the next page and be careful that no one else sees it."

Pip's chair screeched against the floorboards as she shuffled it back to the table.

"Wait, can I go for a piss before we do the next bit?" Ant asked. "I'm bursting."

Jamie nodded. "Yep, sure. The rest can be reading their secrets while we wait."

Pip's heart dragged its way up to her throat as she snatched up her booklet. What was her biggest secret? What exactly was Celia Bourne hiding?

She turned the page.

YOUR SECRET

You are not who you say you are, Celia Bourne. You have been lying this entire time; you are not a governess.

You are a **spy**, working for His Majesty's Secret Service. A few weeks ago, you were approached by a handler and offered a handsome sum and a permanent future position if you investigated your uncle, Reginald Remy. The government suspected that he was connected to communists and may have been involved in seditious activity. They think he might have recently paid a lot of money to a miner and known communist agitator, Harris Pick.

Your mission was to find evidence of this money transfer.

It was **YOU** who broke into the safe after leaving the library and before Reginald returned to his study at 5:15 p.m.

KILL JOY GAMES™

You stole Reginald's checkbook from the safe. There was nothing else in there, certainly not the new will. When Ralph overheard you on the phone, you were speaking in code to your handler.

YOU MUST KEEP THIS SECRET.

If anyone finds out that it was you who broke into the safe, you must lie about your reasons. Tell them that you were simply looking for an old photograph of your mother and you believed your uncle kept it in his safe. You only took the checkbook because you wanted to see how much Reginald was paying other family members, as you have always felt bitter about this.

KILL JOY GAMES™

Pip put her booklet facedown, refusing to glance up in case anyone was watching her and somehow read the secret across her face. Stole it from her head out through her eyes. Stupid, she knew, but still, she didn't look.

A spy. She'd sensed her secret was pretty big, but a government spy? That changed everything. And during that phone conversation with her handler, Ralph had overheard her saying the word *terminate*. What if she'd been given orders to take Reginald Remy out if she found evidence of his treason? What if she was the murderer? Could she have done it? Did Celia Bourne have it in her?

She tuned back into the room and the others had resumed talking. Maybe it was safe to look up now. No one was watching her, but she felt watched anyway somehow, hairs prickling at the back of her neck.

"Can I just check my phone for two seconds, Connor?" Lauren was asking. "Tom's probably texting me and wondering why I'm ignoring him."

"No," Cara answered instead. "He knows you're at a murder mystery party. You can go a few hours without contacting your boyfriend. You'll live, I'm sure. I mean, unless you murdered Reginald Remy, in which case they'll probably hang you."

"OK, has everyone read their secrets?" Jamie said. "Oh, wait . . . Ant's not back yet."

Connor sniffed and stared at the open door. "He's been gone a while. He hasn't drunk enough to pass out, has he? I'll go check on him." He sidled out of the room, and his footsteps were lost beneath the music. But it wasn't quite loud enough to cover the sound of the wind outside, whistling against the house, slamming the shed door.

Pip turned to the windows, but it was completely black out there now. All she could see was their own reflection, Cara making bunny ears over Pip's head and the dancing flames of the candles. She locked eyes with the mirror-image Pip, trapped in the darkness of outside, until she saw Connor's reflection return.

"I can't find Ant," he said. "I checked the downstairs and upstairs bathrooms. He's not there. He's gone."

"What?" Pip said. "Well, he must be somewhere."

"He's not. I've checked everywhere."

"Everywhere?"

"Well, no, not every room."

Jamie pushed up to his feet, taking charge. "Come on, Con," he said. "Let's go look again."

The brothers left the dining room and Jamie's voice sailed through the house.

"Ant?! Where've you gone, you little shit?"

Cara turned to Pip. "What's going on?" she asked, abandoning her Dora voice.

"I don't know." Those three words Pip hated to say.

"He can't have actually gone anywhere," Zach said, but even he didn't sound sure.

"Ant?!" Connor's shout was softened by the carpets and walls, but there was a new urgency to it. "Ant! ANT!" The word grew louder and louder as Connor made his way back to them, Jamie right behind him.

There was an awkward, expectant silence. And the music felt different somehow, changed; the climbing notes of the trumpets now sounded like a threat.

"Yeah, he's, er . . . he's not here," Jamie said. "We looked in every room."

"He's gone?" Lauren fiddled nervously with her beaded necklace. "How is he gone?"

Pip stood up. She wasn't going anywhere, but sitting didn't feel right anymore. From the corner of her eye she saw her dark mirror image get to her feet too, side-glancing back at her. No wonder she felt watched.

"How could he have left? We would have heard the front door," Cara said, looking to Jamie, who could only reply with a shrug.

"Connor, you need to unlock our phones," Lauren said, "so we can call Ant."

"How're we going to call him when I also have *his* phone?" Connor replied, a small bite to his tone.

As she watched the reflected scene unfold in the window, an idea took hold in Pip's mind. This whole thing . . .

it was a performance. A game. It wasn't real, just like those mirror people in their 1920s getups.

"Jamie," Pip said, "is this part of the game? Ant going missing?"

"No, it isn't," he replied, his face giving away nothing.

"Was it something in Bobby's booklet?" she said, her eyes seeking it out, discarded on Ant's plate. "Did it tell him to hide? Is he the next person to be murdered?"

"No," Jamie said, raising his hands earnestly, no hint of amusement in his eyes. "I swear this is not part of the game. This isn't supposed to happen. I promise."

She believed him, picking up on the growing unease in the lines on Jamie's face.

"Where could he have gone? It's dark outside." Pip gestured to the window. "And he doesn't have his phone. Something's not right."

"What do I do?" Jamie asked the room. He seemed to shrink, almost, lose six years until he was just one of them. "I don't—"

But Pip didn't hear what he said next.

The room erupted with a sharp pounding coming from the window.

There was someone out there. Someone unseen. Knocking on the window. Again and again. Faster and faster. So hard that the pane seemed to shake in its frame.

"Oh my god!" Lauren screamed, scrambling back to the far wall, her chair clattering to the floor.

Pip couldn't see anything. It was too dark out there and too bright in here. All she saw was their own reflection, their fear-widened eyes. They were blind in here. Trapped. And someone was out there, someone who could see everything.

Pip watched Cara's reflection grabbing for her hand before she felt it.

The knocking picked up, louder and faster, and Pip's heart beat harder and harder to match it, trying to escape her chest. Too fast; maybe there was more than one someone out there?

And, just as sudden, the knocking cut out. The glass stopped shaking. But Pip could feel it still, as though the knocking was inside her now, hiding at the base of her throat.

"Wh—" Connor started to say, his voice shaking at the edges.

Then the outside flooded with light, blazing through the window at them, and Pip covered her eyes against the glare.

eight

"What the—"

Pip blinked until her eyes could focus on the light streaming in from the yard and the shape silhouetted against it.

She blinked again and the shape grew arms and legs. A person standing there just outside the window.

It was Ant.

A sheepish look on his face above his stupid mustache as he searched over his shoulder for the motion-sensor floodlight he must have tripped.

"For fuck's sake." Jamie sounded annoyed, whacking his booklet against the table and turning to his brother.

Connor exhaled. "I'm sorry. He's always like this, pulling pranks."

"Well, can he do it on his own time?" Jamie said. "Now we might not have time to finish before everyone gets picked up."

"Yeah, sorry, Jamie. Sorry, I know you've put a lot of effort into tonight." Connor turned to the window and shouted, "Ant, come back inside! You fucking loon," he added under his breath as Ant stepped away from the window toward the door to the kitchen, where he must have snuck out.

"Soooo not funny," Lauren said, righting her chair and sitting back down.

"Hey, guys," Ant said breathlessly as he reentered the dining room. "Oh god, that was so funny; you should have seen your faces. Lauren, you looked like you shit yourself."

"Fuck off," she said, but her face had already cracked into a smile. Way to hold out.

"And, Pip"—Ant turned to her—"you kept looking, like, directly at me. I thought you could see me."

"Hmm" was all the reply she gave, scolding her heart, trying to force it back down.

"Well," said Zach, "at least it *was* just a prank and Ant hasn't been brutally murdered by an intruder."

Always the peacemaker, Zach. Though Pip wasn't sure she entirely agreed with him right now.

"Anyway," Jamie said, raising his voice, "we need to get on with it or we'll never bring this murderer to justice. If Bobby Remy has stopped fucking around, let's continue." He opened his master booklet and scanned his eyes across it. "Right, OK. So now that you've all learned your own greatest secrets, the ones you must protect at all costs, it's time to spill some other secrets you might know about your fellow suspects. Everyone please sit down and turn to the next page in your booklet."

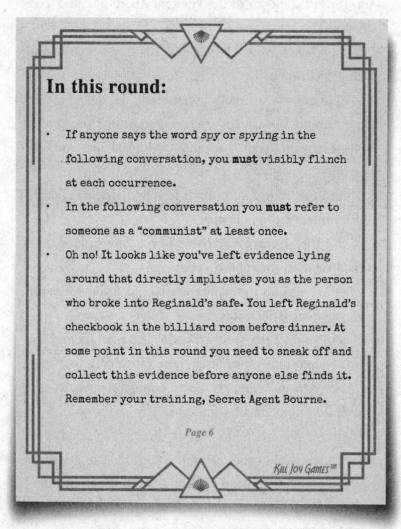

In this round:

- If anyone says the word *spy* or *spying* in the following conversation, you **must** visibly flinch at each occurrence.
- In the following conversation you **must** refer to someone as a "communist" at least once.
- Oh no! It looks like you've left evidence lying around that directly implicates you as the person who broke into Reginald's safe. You left Reginald's checkbook in the billiard room before dinner. At some point in this round you need to sneak off and collect this evidence before anyone else finds it. Remember your training, Secret Agent Bourne.

Page 6

KILL JOY GAMES™

What? Pip read that last point again. Why would she leave evidence just lying around? What kind of dumbass spy was Celia Bourne? Pip would never be so stupid. And now she had to go and fix it before she got caught.

The closet in the hallway, that was the billiard room. How would Pip leave the dining room without raising the others' suspicions, though? Especially after the stunt Ant just pulled.

"Well"—Connor spoke as Humphrey, the butler—"if we are talking about secrets, I suppose I might know one. A particularly juicy one."

"Do spill, old Hump," said Cara.

"I don't mean to be improper"—Connor bowed his head—"and I certainly wasn't spying."

Pip flinched, and she didn't really have to act it, surprised the word had come up so soon. Her wrist knocked into her glass, but she caught it before it toppled, catching Connor's eye. "Sorry," she whispered.

"It was yesterday, late afternoon, and as I was walking through the house, doing my butlering duties, I heard . . . well, from one of the bedrooms upstairs I heard a man and a woman, um . . . well, I believe I heard *relations* going on."

Ant snorted.

"Well, we do have a married couple staying here. Ralph and Lizzie." Pip gestured to Zach and Lauren across the table.

"Yes, very good, ma'am." Connor bowed again. "Except I was making my way toward the lounge when I heard these . . . *relations* . . . and young master Ralph was in the lounge at the time, playing chess with his father."

Cara supplied the gasp again, pointing at Lauren.

"Why are you pointing at me?" Lauren looked aghast. "It could have been any one of us."

"Very unlikely to be me, as I'm a lowly cook and one hundred years old," Cara replied.

"Well, it could have been Pip—Celia, I mean."

"Hmm, no it couldn't," Pip thought aloud. "If Humphrey, Ralph Remy, and Reginald Remy were all downstairs at the time, there's only one man it could have been: Bobby."

They all turned to Ant, who attempted to keep a straight face, stroking his mustache thoughtfully.

"Yeah, so maybe it was Pip and Ant!" Lauren said, louder than needed.

"Bobby Remy is my cousin," Pip reminded her.

"W-well, s-s-so," Lauren spluttered. "Incest is a thing."

"I think thou doth protest too much, Lizzie dear," Pip said, clicking her pen in a way she hoped was annoying. "It's pretty clear who those *relations* were between. Nice to see you're so close to your brother-in-law. Oh"—she turned to Zach—"sorry, Ralph. Must be hard for you to hear."

Zach smiled. "I'm devastated."

"Well, I fiercely deny it," Lauren said, looking embarrassed, shuffling her chair farther away from Ant. Art imitating life, Pip thought. "The butler must be mistaken. He *is* old; we can't trust his hearing. And why are we all turning on each other? It's ridiculous."

"All right, *communist,*" Pip said.

It didn't quite work there, but where else was she going to fit it in?

"You know what, fine," Lauren spat, crossing her arms. "Fuck you, butler—"

"My name's Humphrey," Connor interrupted, tapping his name badge.

"Whatever you're called," she said. "Because I know you happen to be keeping secrets yourself. I've seen you twice this weekend taking a piece of paper out of your pocket and staring at it. I even caught you crying one time. What is it? What is this secret note that you're carrying around, huh?"

"I don't know what note you are talking about, madam," Connor said.

"Oh, do you mean *this* note?" Jamie was on his feet, standing behind his brother's chair. He leaned over him and snaked his hand down the inside of Connor's tuxedo, pulling out a folded piece of paper from his inside pocket.

"Jamie, what?!" Connor said, beaming up at his brother in disbelief. "When the hell did you sneak that in there?"

"I have my ways." Jamie smiled, brandishing the folded

note. Pip could see the words *Clue #3* printed on the back. "Well, well, well," he said, opening it. "Thanks to your sharp eyes, Lizzie." He feigned reading it. "Interesting. Here, pass this around." Jamie handed the note to Pip first, Connor leaning in to read it over her shoulder.

Smallpox (*variola virus*)

Smallpox is a highly contagious and frequently fatal disease. It is characterized by high fever and a distinctive rash that leaves pustules all over the body. Transmission occurs via the respiratory tract through air droplets.

In fatal cases death will likely occur between 10–16 days after the initial onset of symptoms.

KILL JOY GAMES™

"Strange," Jamie commented as Pip passed the clue to Cara. "It looks to be a page ripped from one of the medical books from Reginald's library."

"'Smallpox,'" Zach read aloud when the page was passed to him.

"It was eradicated by the nineteen eighties," Pip said.

"Oi, no time travel." Jamie whacked her on the head with his master booklet.

"Why do you have this in your pocket?" Lauren asked Connor as the paper made its way into her hands. "And why do you keep looking at it?"

"No reason," Connor said, his already pink cheeks flushing a darker shade. "I am just interested in the topic, that's all. I sometimes like to read to pass the time, though the master never approved of that, called it idleness. That's why I hide it."

"Sounds very un-legit to me," Cara said.

Connor opened his mouth to say more, but then he forced it shut and shrugged instead; clearly he had nothing else to offer on the matter. Maybe now was a good time for Pip to sneak off to the billiard room to find and hide the incriminating evidence. She put down her pen and was just about to speak when Ant cut across her. Damn, missed her chance.

"You know what," he said as Bobby, a wagging finger accompanying his words. "I've been thinking this all weekend, and now, sitting across from you, I'm almost sure." He turned to stare at Cara. "I recognize you from somewhere, Dora Key. I'm certain this isn't the first time we've met."

"Oh, don't tell me we've hooked up too," she quipped, pretending to scour her booklet for the offending line.

"No, but I've definitely seen you somewhere . . . somewhere." He pretended to search his memory, fingering the sides of his mustache like a caricature. And then it clicked, and his face changed.

"Remembered, have you?" Cara said. "I recognize you too, from *somewhere.* Pretty foolish of you to bring it up, Bobby. Doesn't look great for either of us."

"I know," Ant said. "But my booklet told me to."

"Ah, that sucks. Maybe we can just keep this mutually damaging secret between us?"

"Nope, not allowed," Jamie intervened with a small chuckle. "Spill. Now."

"OK, fine." Ant held up his hands. "I recognize you from the Garza casino in London. I've seen you there a few times, hanging around with the Garza family. I know it's you. I recognize the, um . . . deep, deep lines painted on your face."

"Ah, thank you. My best feature," Cara replied.

"Wait," Lauren said. "Why would a lowly cook be hanging around in a high-end casino?"

A good question for once. Pip and her pen waited.

"Judgmental," said Cara. "Poor people like to gamble too. This was before I was employed by Reginald Remy and moved here, so I don't see how it's any of your business. And, anyway, why are you focusing on me? Bobby was also there. And what's more"—Cara leaned forward—"I've seen him there multiple times, hanging around with a known gang. And once I even saw him selling small packets of white powder to casino-goers."

"Sounds like cocaine," Jamie said, knocking his police hat.

"Wait," Zach waded in now, turning to speak to Ant. "Bobby, you've been going to the Garza casino, our rivals? Our enemies?"

"Well, it's not like I can walk into any Remy casino in the country, can I? I was permanently banned."

"So you've been gambling again?" Zach looked genuinely betrayed. "You didn't give it up, even though you promised Father and the rest of us years ago that you would never do it again?"

"Guilty," Ant said, pressing one hand to his pin-striped chest.

"Father promised to cut you off if you ever gambled again. Did he find out?"

"Nope."

"Did Mother? She was friendly with Mr. Garza's wife before her death. Maybe Mrs. Garza told her."

"Nope," Ant said again.

Zach's face furrowed, a shadow falling across his eyes. Ralph didn't believe his brother, Pip could tell.

"*And* you were dealing cocaine?" Pip zeroed in on Ant.

"What, you believe the word of a cook? Come on, cousin,

I know we all love to hate on Bobby, but Dora is clearly just trying to deflect from why she was there. Which is very suspicious in itself."

Well, he wasn't wrong there either. Why had Dora Key been seen frequenting a high-end casino, hanging around with the Remys' main business rivals?

There was a lull, a natural dip in the confrontation, and if Pip didn't go now, she might not get another chance.

"Hey, can we pause for a second?" she said, closing her notebook so the others couldn't peek at her growing number of theories. "I need to pee."

Jamie nodded. "Yep, sure."

"Where're you going?" Cara demanded, standing up too.

"I just said." Pip turned back at the threshold. "To pee. And I won't pull a disappearing act like Ant, don't worry."

"Can I come with you?" Cara said, drawing forward.

"No." Pip's heart picked up against her ribs. Cara was going to ruin everything. She *had* to get to that evidence now. "I'm just going to the bathroom, you weirdo," she said, her palms starting to sweat, hoping that was enough to keep Cara at bay. She hated lying, especially to Cara, who was more of a sister than a friend.

But it worked. Cara relented, and Pip strolled out of the dining room alone, down the hallway. She opened the door to the downstairs bathroom and closed it loudly so the others would hear, even over the music. But Pip wasn't inside. She continued down the hall, pressing her feet as quietly as she could into the carpet.

She drew to a stop outside the closet and the gently swaying sign that read *Billiard Room.*

Pip reached for the handle, noticing a tremor in her fingers. Why was she nervous? This wasn't even real, none of it. But it didn't feel that way, and she felt different too, somehow. More alive, more aware, her skin thrumming and electric. She pulled the closet open, and there on the floor, before a rack of shoes, was something that hadn't been there before: a folded piece of paper with the words *Clue #4.*

She bent down and stretched out her hand to take the clue.

But she never made it.

Her fingers only skimmed it before someone grabbed her from behind.

nine

Unseen hands on her shoulders. Fingers digging in, pulling her away.

Pip overbalanced and fell, landing on her back. And finally, she could see who had grabbed her.

"Cara, what the hell are you doing?" she said, scrambling up.

But it was too late.

Cara had swooped in, head inside the closet, her fingers closing around the paper. She turned back, holding up the clue, a wide grin on her face.

"I *knew* you were sneaking off to do something naughty," she said, poking Pip in the ribs with her other hand.

"How on earth did you know?"

"Well, my booklet told me you were," Cara said. "Told me you were going to sneak off and that I had to catch you and find some *evidence* before you destroyed it."

"Urgh." Pip pushed up to her feet, disentangling her arms from the feather boa. Stupid game, setting her up to fail like that. "Well, at least now we know you don't just want to watch me pee."

"Not my thing, sorry," Cara said. "Here you go." She outstretched her hand, offering the clue back to Pip.

Pip reached for it. Just within her grasp. And then Cara whipped it away again, hiding it behind her back.

"LOL, joke," she giggled, backing away toward the dining room.

Pip took her revenge, prodding Cara in the armpit.

"Ouch, that was my boob!" Cara butt-shoved Pip into the wall.

"What's going on out there?!" Ant's voice called. "Is it a girl fight?"

Cara broke free from Pip and ran back to the dining room, holding the clue in the air. "Pi—sorry, Celia was trying to hide this!" she announced to them all, Pip traipsing in behind her.

"Only because the game told me to," Pip said defensively, retaking her seat and crossing her arms.

"Ah, not such a good girl, are we?" Ant teased her.

"What is it, Dora?" Jamie asked. "Open it and pass it around the table."

"What is it?" Zach asked.

"It's a checkbook, belonging to Reginald Remy," Cara

said. "And the most recent stub shows a payment to some-one called Harris Pick. Old Reggie paid him one hundred and fifty K at the end of July."

Date: 22/07/1924

To Harris Pick: to settle a long overdue debt

£ 150,000

CHEQUE

YOUR NAME

£

PAY TO THE ORDER OF

POUNDS

AUTHORIZED SIGNATURE   DATE

324297797423 436346

Ant whistled, impressed by the figure.

"Wait a minute," Zach said, his voice unnaturally level as he read directly from his booklet. "I recognize that name. He and my father served in the First Boer War to-gether. Father always said that Harris saved his life."

It was also the name of the communist agitator that the government suspected Reginald Remy of funding. And here was Celia's proof: one hundred and fifty thousand pounds. That was *a lot* of money; must have been millions in today's terms.

"Yes, well"—Cara shot a scathing look at Pip, a smile hiding underneath—"I saw Celia coming out of Reginald's study at about five this evening, holding the checkbook. *She* was the one who broke into the safe and stole this!"

"Celia?" There was a troubled look in Zach's eyes.

"Yes, OK," Pip sighed. "I did. It was me who broke into the safe. But it's not how it looks. I was just looking for a photograph Reginald had of my mother. I didn't see it anywhere in the house, so I thought he must keep in it his safe. I just wanted to see if I look like her now."

"Oh, boo-hoo, spare us the sob story," Ant said. "If that's the case, why did you steal the checkbook?"

"Well, when I opened the safe, there was nothing in there except that." Pip pointed to the paper in Cara's hands. "And I guess I wanted to know how much money my uncle sends to his children, and their plus-ones." She glared at Lauren. "I've always been bitter about that. I was an orphan and he could have helped me, but he always chose not to."

"Interesting," Jamie said, the inspector stepping in. "So, Celia, we can now place you at the scene of the murder only fifteen minutes before it potentially happened."

It wasn't looking good for her.

"Yes, but," Pip protested, "Dora just said she saw me coming out of the study at five, which means I left the scene well before the time of the murder. And why was *she* up there? You made this whole deal about going to the vegetable patch at that time. So you must be lying too."

"Yes, thank you." Zach excitedly slapped the table. "Dora, you weren't even there to *not see* me on my walk and throw doubt on my alibi."

"And why were you heading toward Reginald's study?" Pip turned on her.

"You know what, I said it to Ralph and I'll say it again," Lauren said. "I don't like that cook; she's always in places she shouldn't be. It's like she's spying on us."

Pip didn't realize at first, flinching at the word a half-second too late. She looked up and again caught Connor's eye; he'd been watching her.

"Looking a little twitchy there, Celia," he remarked.

"Right." Jamie clapped his hands. "We are getting very close to the truth; soon we will uncover who among you is the murderer. But first I think the killer needs to admit it to themselves. So if you look under your plates—wait, Connor, let me explain first—you will find an envelope with your name on it. Inside will be a piece of paper that will tell you if you are the killer or not. But"—he raised a finger to underline the point—"you must keep a poker face. Don't give anything away, whether you're the murderer or not." He eyeballed them all to make sure they understood, his gaze lingering longest on Ant. "OK, go."

Pip slid her plate forward, an uneaten pizza slice discarded on it that she knew Connor had his eye on. And there, hidden underneath this entire time, was a small envelope with her name on it: *Celia Bourne.*

She glanced at the others, already tearing into their envelopes, and reached for her own.

She stalled. Withdrew her fingers, balling them up into a fist.

What if she *was* the murderer? She had a cold, sinking feeling in her gut. Celia was at the murder scene only fifteen minutes before the time-of-death window. What if she'd seen the check stub to Harris Pick—evidence of Reginald's treason—and, under orders from her handler, had returned to the study to *terminate* her uncle? A knife through the heart. She'd never felt welcomed into the Remy family, not really. Maybe her rage took over, or maybe it was her training. Either way, a man was dead, and she might have killed him. The answer was right here.

Pip picked up the envelope, lifted the flap, and pulled out the folded piece of paper. She held it close as she opened it, heart in her throat as she read the words printed there.

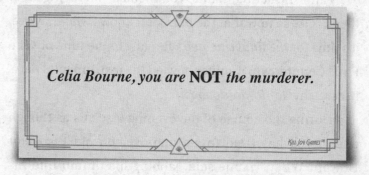

Celia Bourne, you are **NOT** *the murderer.*

KILL JOY GAMES™

She read it again, just to be sure, the voice in her head overenunciating every syllable. She wasn't the killer, thank god. Celia didn't do it. She was innocent.

Pip watched as the others rearranged their faces to hide their secrets. Connor was waggling his eyebrows in an unnatural formation of one-up, two-up, one-down, two-down. Lauren was giggling, glancing side to side. Ant studied the ceiling. Cara's eyes were so comically wide as she stared everyone down that—alongside the face paint wrinkles—it looked a little like her eye sockets had cracked open. Zach was silent, straining to keep his face neutral.

If it wasn't her, then someone at this table was the murderer. One of her five friends. And who could it be? Every single one of them had opportunity and means. And now Pip had seven pages of notes about all of them, why they might have killed Reginald Remy. They all looked guilty in her eyes, but it could only be one.

"Fantastic acting," Jamie commented, surveying all of them. "OK, so now that the murderer knows who they are, it's time for *the final clue-ooo*," he sang to the tune of "The Final Countdown." Connor howled the instrumental parts in scratchy *do-do-do-doooo*s.

"During the course of the evening it seems as though one of you has tried to get one over on old Inspector Howard Whey," Jamie said, jabbing his thumb into his chest. "Someone has tried to throw out an incriminating piece of evidence in a place none of us would think to look. Trying to disguise it among the waste from this very dinner."

"Huh?" Connor said, one eyebrow climbing his fore-head again as he stared at his brother, confused.

Pip followed Jamie's eyes to the center of the table. The three red candles flickered away, and there was their growing pile of clues, a few empty bottles of red wine and the beers Connor had been drinking. Their plates were empty, apart from Pip's because there'd been too much thinking to do to concentrate on eating. What did Jamie mean? What had changed here?

And then it clicked. What had been in the middle of the table before and was now missing.

"The pizza boxes!" Pip stood up.

Jamie shrugged, but there was a playful smile tugging on the corners of his mouth.

"Where are they? By the recycling bins?" Connor asked, but Jamie was giving nothing more away.

"Come on," Connor said to them all, rushing out of the dining room toward the kitchen, Pip right on his heels, notebook in hand.

The Domino's boxes had been piled up in the corner, tucked beside the recycling bin. Connor got to his knees—miming discomfort because of Humphrey Todd's advanced age—and started pulling them out, opening their cardboard lids as the rest of the group sidled in behind.

"Aha," he said, holding up a piece of paper, which now had a little bit of garlic dip and pizza grease smeared across it. On the back Pip saw the words *Final Clue*.

"See, nothing passes under the nose of Inspector Howard Whey," Jamie said triumphantly. "Please share the note with the group, Humphrey."

> Tonight. Before dinner. You promised me. We both want this, and it's too late to go back after everything we've already done. It will all be fine. Remember: he does not deserve our sympathy.
>   I will see you later.
>   -RR

"Ooh, juicy," Connor said. "Literally," as he wiped the pizza juice off his fingers.

"RR," Lauren said. "Well, it must be from one of you two." She turned to the Remy brothers.

"And Bobby already left a note today signed off as RR, Robert Remy," Pip said, but there was something in her head, some under-formed thought she couldn't yet grasp. What was it? What was bugging her about this note?

"Sounds like the kind of note someone might send to their brother's wife that they're screwing behind his back," Cara said. "Did you two plan to have more *relations* this evening?" she asked Lauren and Ant.

Pip considered that for a moment. She supposed it worked; but something didn't feel right in her gut.

"Or does it sound like two people were planning the murder together? Two killers!" Connor said excitedly.

Pip considered that too. That could also fit, in the context of the note. Her mind whirred.

"As the genius inspector I am," Jamie said, "I can confirm that only one of the six of you is our murderer. And now"—he clapped his hands loudly—"it is finally time to unmask the killer. To reveal the whole truth and nothing but the truth. If you would all like to retake your seats in the dining room." He gestured them back across the corridor.

They stumbled out of the kitchen, the others discussing the murder in quick, excitable sound bites, exchanging theories. But Pip was silent, alone in her thoughts. Running the case through her head from the start to the very end, like Celia Bourne might have done. Dissecting every clue, looking at it from a different angle.

The six of them took their seats at the table once more. Pip turned straight to her notebook, frantically flipping through the pages and her increasingly erratic handwriting. So many suspects, so many reasons to have wanted Reginald Remy dead. But who did it? Who among them was the killer? All the signs seemed to be pointing one way, to Robert "Bobby" Remy. Since the very beginning so many of the clues had cast deep shadows over him.

Almost too many, and something about it didn't feel right. She was missing something.

Pip had just started writing out a list of their character names to cross them out one by one. And then the world went black, stolen from her eyes.

Everything swallowed by darkness as all the lights blinked out. The music died, leaving an unnerving, buzzing silence in its wake.

It shattered a second later as someone screamed.

ten

"Lauren, stop screaming" came Connor's panicked voice somewhere off to the right.

Pip's eyes readjusted, making themselves at home in the darkness. She wasn't entirely sightless; the three candles in front gave off a weak pool of flickering orange light, and Pip could just about separate the rough outlines of her friends from the other shadows.

A new faceless silhouette joined them, hanging in the doorway, its head overgrown and distorted.

"What did you guys do?" the shadow asked in Jamie's voice.

"We didn't do anything," Connor replied.

"Ah, fuck, must be a power cut," he said, shifting on his feet, a ripple in the dark.

"Not a power cut," Pip said, her own voice feeling strange to her, cutting through the unnatural silence. "Look, out there." She pointed to the window, forgetting she was just an indistinct shape in the darkness. "You can see the lights from your neighbor's windows; they still have power. Must be a blown fuse."

"Ah," Jamie said. "Did you plug anything in?"

"No." Connor's voice again. "We were just sitting here. Alexa was on."

"It's fine—we just need to reset the fuse box." Pip fumbled, getting to her feet. "Do you know where it is? Is it outside?"

"No, it's in the basement, I think," Jamie said. "I don't know. I never go down there."

"Because it's creepy AF," Connor added unhelpfully.

"Have you ever reset a fuse box before?" she asked. The silence from the Reynolds brothers was answer enough. No one else stepped up either. "Fine," she sighed. "I'll do it."

If Pip's dad were here, he'd be vigorously shaking his head right now; fuse boxes were one of his very first *Life Lessons.* Granted, Pip probably hadn't needed to be taught that at age nine, but a "life lesson was for life" as he always said. Don't even get him started about checking the oil in the car.

"Won't you need a flashlight or something?" Connor asked.

"Oh, Connor," Lauren said, almost invisible across the

table, "you should unlock our phones so we can use the flashlights on them."

"Yeah, fine," Connor said over the rasping sound of him getting up from his chair. "It's not very 1924, but fine." Muffled footsteps and then a new sound: his hands scrabbling around the radiator, the metal clanging much louder than it should. "Crap," he hissed. "I can't find the key. I know I left it here somewhere."

"For fuck's sake, Connor!" Lauren again. "I need my phone."

"It's fine, it's fine," Pip said, defusing the situation. She leaned across the table and picked up one of the candlesticks, the flame dancing in her breath. "This is fine; I can see enough. You can find the key once the lights are back on." She used the shaky firelight to navigate around Jamie in the doorway.

"Do you need help?" he asked her.

"No, no, that's OK." She knew he was anxious about finishing the game before they all had to go, but this was really a job for one person. Pip found that—most of the time—other people only slowed you down. That was why she despised group projects. "I'll just be a second. No worries."

She'd never been down to the Reynoldses' basement before, but there was only one door it could be. One that was unlabeled and played no part in the make-believe

Remy Manor. The door under the stairs. She lowered the candle to find the knob and grabbed it, the metal cold, stinging her skin.

"I think it's in the back left-hand corner," the Jamie outline told her.

"Got it," she said, pulling the door open.

It creaked. Of course it frickin' creaked, the sound echoing in the dark hall, riding along her nerves. *Get it together, Pip. It's just an old, hardly used door.*

Before her was an opening, so impossibly dark that her eyes brought it to life and the shadows breached the threshold, creeping out to take her, make her one of them. Kept at bay only by the small flame she held up. There must be a staircase here, she knew that, feeling the top stair out with her shoe before she stepped down it. Losing her feet to the darkness.

The air was colder and staler down here, and it only seemed to grow darker with every step, her candle losing the battle.

The fourth step down creaked. Of course.

Pip's heart spiked at the sound, though her head told her she was being ridiculous. All the murder talk must have put her on edge.

On the sixth step something brushed against her bare arm. Something delicate that prickled at her skin, like the gentle brush of fingers. She swiped at it. A cobweb. It clung on, holding on to her hand, catching her. Pip wiped it on her dress and moved on.

She shifted her foot, ready for another step, but it wasn't there. Just more ground. She'd reached the bottom, in the basement now, a shiver passing up the back of her neck. She turned to check that the way back still existed: the lighter shape of the hall door was still up there. She swore to god if someone thought it would be funny to lock her down here, there might actually be a murder tonight.

A rustle behind her.

Pip turned, the flame overstretching to keep up with her.

She couldn't see anything, except . . . Yes, she could. Over there in the corner, it was the fuse box, just a few feet away. She traced her steps over to it, lifting the candle to light it up. All the switches had flipped down, including the main red one on the end.

Her fingers stalled in the air. There was a whisper in the darkness. To her right. Had she really heard something? She couldn't be sure, the sound of her heart too loud in her ears.

Pip held the candle high to light as much of the underground room as she could.

That was when she saw the man.

Standing in the other corner, the dark shape of his head tilted like he was watching her, curiously.

"Wh-who's there?" Pip said, her voice shaking.

He didn't answer. The wind did instead, whistling in through hidden cracks somewhere above her.

Pip's fingers shook, the fire juddering with them, and the man moved. Coming toward her.

"No!"

She spun back to the fuse box. She needed the lights, needed them now. She had only a few seconds before . . .

She focused, grip tight on the candle, her breath quickening, in and out and . . . Oh no. The darkness was complete, caving in on her, wrapping her up. She'd blown out the candle. Oh shit, oh fuck, oh no.

Blindly, she fumbled at the fuse box, flicking unseen switches with her thumb. Up, up, up, up. Her fingers found the wider shape of the main switch and she pushed it.

The lights came on and the shadow man was gone.

Gone, because he was actually just a haphazard pile of cardboard boxes with a sheet thrown over them. It was only Pip down here, although it took a few seconds for her heart to trust her.

She heard cheering and whooping upstairs from the others.

"Well done, Pip!" Jamie's voice called. "Come on back up!"

She might just take a few deep breaths first, wait for the fear to drain from her face. What had gotten into her? It was just a basement, disorganized and dusty. But hold on, why could she see it at all? Why had the light been on down here anyway? That was weird.

Back to the staircase, all of its shadows filled in now. One hand holding the spent candle, the other on the banister, she walked up, avoiding the rest of the cobwebs. And then something she didn't expect to see, staring her in the face. An envelope tucked between two of the staircase posts at the creaky fourth step. An envelope with *A SECRET CLUE, JUST FOR YOU* written on it.

Wait a second—what?

Pip picked it up, checking it was real.

It was. The words *Kill Joy Games*™ formed a faint border around its edge.

She exhaled and her breath changed in her throat, became a shaky laugh.

Sneaky Jamie Reynolds.

None of this had been real. None of the last few minutes.

It was all part of the game: the blackout, Jamie pretending he didn't know what to do with a fuse box. A fuse probably hadn't even blown; Jamie must have been down here, flipping the switches off himself while they were all waiting, unknowing, in the dining room. The whole thing was made up to get someone down here on their own. And that person had earned themselves their own bonus clue.

It was hers.

Pip grinned, tearing into it, running her eyes across the page.

Congratulations! This secret final clue is yours and yours alone; you do not have to share it with the group if you choose not to.

Over the last few months a doctor has been regularly visiting Remy Manor. No one knew about this at the time, not the family or the staff. The prognosis wasn't good. Reginald Remy had cancer of the lungs. He was not expected to live much longer; he certainly wouldn't make it to his seventy-fifth birthday.

A couple of weeks ago the doctor was paid a large sum of money to keep quiet about Reginald's condition.

Do what you will with this information.

Kill Joy Games™

The world halted around Pip, dust hanging motionless in the air around her head, the secret crumpling in her hands. Reginald Remy had been dying, and he knew it. But he hadn't wanted anyone else to know. This changed everything. The whole case. This was it, the new angle she'd needed. The story that had been hiding there all along, stirring that feeling in her gut. It all came together, the suspects reshuffling before her eyes and—

Jamie called for her again.

"Coming," she said, reaching the top of the stairs, sliding the paper under the shoulder of her dress, tucking it into her bra strap.

She walked into the dining room, the others waiting for her. As she took her seat, releasing the candlestick, she caught Jamie's eye and the small secret smile in his pursed lips. She returned a discreet nod.

"OK," Jamie said, stepping back into the role of Inspector Howard Whey. "Now it really is time for the truth. And time for you to all make your final guesses. Who is the murderer? Please turn to the last page in your booklets."

WELL DONE, CELIA BOURNE.

You have survived this night of murder, mystery, and mayhem.

It's time to answer the ultimate question:

Who murdered Reginald Remy?

Please write your answer in the spaces below.

The killer is: _____

Their motive is: _____

_____

_____

_____

_____

KILL JOY GAMES ™

eleven

Pip knew.

She knew who the killer was.

Every piece slotted into place in her head, all those near-forgotten details right from the start that had come through the blackout into a new light. The clues, and not just what they said but how they said it. Not the words, but the shape of them. The font. She looked at everyone in the room, playing it out in her head as her eyes flitted from suspect to suspect. The killer in this room, in this manor, on this secluded island where the boat came only once a day.

The truth had been hiding there all along, riding on the underbelly of all those obvious clues and secrets. God, she'd been naive to fall for them at the time. Of course it would never be that obvious, that easy; this was a murder, after all. But she had it all now, the entire writhing thing: every twist and every turn. And she needed far more than four little lines to capture it all.

"Right"—Jamie leaned into his elbows—"let's go around the table and everyone share their theories before I reveal the truth. Lauren? Want to start us off?"

"OK," she said, fidgeting with her beaded necklace, pulling it tighter around her neck. "So I think the murderer is . . . Cara. Dora, the cook, I mean." She paused as Cara supplied her signature gasp, looking offended. "I think she's got something to do with our business rivals, the Garzas, and she's here under false pretenses and was sent to steal business secrets and then kill my father-in-law."

She was correct on some of that, Pip conceded. But not the most important part.

"Ant, your guess?" Jamie said.

"Well, the only murderer around here is . . . Sal Singh," he said with a grin. "Must be his ghost. Andie Bell and now poor Reginald Remy."

"Ant!" Cara slid forward, attempting to kick him under the table.

"Ouch, OK, OK." He held up his hands in defeat. "Um, I'm going to go for . . . Pip. What's your name again?"

"Celia," she said, glaring back at him.

"Yeah, Celia. I reckon we've got a case here of a good girl gone bad. And I think it would annoy Pip most to be the murderer. So, yeah."

"Such sound reasoning," Jamie said, a hint of annoyance in his tone. "Next."

100

Zach's turn. Pip watched him carefully as he cleared his throat.

"I think the murderer is my brother, Bobby Remy," he said, keeping his eyes to himself. "Bobby never gave up gambling, and I think my mother found out about it. I think she confronted him on that fateful walk one year ago today. And I think my brother murdered her, pushed her off the cliff."

Yes, Pip was right. Ralph Remy had always suspected his brother of killing their mother.

"He's murdered before and I think he murdered again," Zach continued. "He knew my father was going to cut him out of the will, and he wanted that money. That's all he's ever seen my father as—a bank. That's why he tried to destroy the new will and stabbed our father through the heart. Oh, and that note about meeting up before dinner, that was from Bobby to my wife, Lizzie. But that was just Bobby trying to give himself an alibi so he could say he was with Lizzie at the time of the murder, even if she denied it."

Wrong, Pip thought. That wasn't it, and that was the whole point. It was something beyond that, between the lines.

"Connor?" Jamie pointed to him.

"Yeah, so I think it might actually be Celia Bourne." He gave Pip a sideways glance. "I think she might be a Russian spy or something, because she kept reacting to that word, and she was trying to hide incriminating evidence. I think she's lying about why she broke into Reginald's safe, and whatever she found in there, something to do with that Harris Pick dude, it then became her mission to *terminate* Reginald Remy."

Pip was impressed with his observational skills, even if he was dead wrong. She ironed out her face, no expression. It was her turn next. She cracked her neck, gearing up for it.

"Cara?" Jamie said, eyes skipping over Pip. Oh, he was letting her go last. Maybe because she was the one with the bonus secret clue, he thought she was most likely to have the solution. And he was right.

"Yeah, so, despite his actor being the most annoying person in the world," Cara said, her painted wrinkles dancing across her face, "I'm going to go for Bobby Remy. Everything points to him, I think. He's having an affair with his brother's wife. He's been gambling and is now seemingly mixed up with gangsters. Like Ralph said, he probably killed his mother too. He's after his inheritance money, that's why he destroyed the new will and killed his dad."

Cara had fallen for it all, exactly as it had been planned.

And now it was Pip's turn.

She got to her feet before Jamie even had a chance to say her name.

"OK, before we get to who is behind this murder," she said, "we first need to discount who is not involved. Yes,

Dora Key"—she gestured to Cara—"is a plant sent by the Garza family. They threatened the last cook to make her quit, and Dora got herself employed here to keep an eye on the Remy business dealings and report back. But she did not murder my uncle Reginald; why would she? There was nothing for her and the Garzas to gain from that."

Lauren looked deflated, so Pip turned to her next. "Lizzie, you certainly don't come out of this looking so rosy. You've been stealing from the Remy family, skimming money from the London casino. Perhaps you were trying to gain some financial security in case your husband found out about you sleeping with his brother and divorced you and you lost everything. Reginald worked out that you were the thief, and maybe you were worried about him going to the authorities. But you are not the murderer, though you are probably relieved he is dead.

"Humphrey Todd"—she turned her eyes to Connor—"you hated Reginald Remy. You even wished him dead. You said the reason was because you asked for time off work to visit your daughter and he denied you. That was true"—she paused—"but it was only part of the truth. The reason you wanted time off two weeks ago was because your daughter—the only family you have left in the whole world—had contracted a deadly disease: smallpox. But Reginald said no, and your daughter died soon after. You never got a chance to say goodbye. That is why you hated him, in the end, and revenge certainly is a strong motive. But you also did not kill Reginald Remy."

By the flush in Connor's cheeks Pip knew she was right on the mark.

"For my own part," she said, hand on her chest, "yes, Humphrey, you are partly right. I am a spy working for His Majesty's Secret Service, and I was instructed to investigate my uncle and whether he was funding seditious communist activity. Harris Pick is a known communist agitator. But I did not murder my uncle, and my mission was misguided. Reginald wasn't funding communists; he was simply settling his outstanding debts. Sending money to an old friend who had saved his life in the war. Because—and here's the kicker, everyone ... Reginald Remy knew he was going to die."

"What?" Lauren and Ant said in unison, the others staring at her.

"Here." She pulled the secret clue from her dress, dropping it in the middle of the table. "A secret clue that was hidden in the basement, for whoever went down to the fuse box. Reginald was dying of lung cancer, and the doctor told him he didn't have much time left. And just a couple of weeks ago the doctor was sent a load of money to keep his mouth shut about this."

"Oh shit," Zach said, casting his eyes down at the clue.

"Oh shit indeed," Pip continued. "And while you are

right, Dora, that everything seems to be pointing to Bobby Remy, there is a precise reason for that. But while the rest of us didn't have alibis for the time of the murder, two people here actually did." She nodded at Lauren and Ant. "Lizzie and Bobby Remy were together at the time of the murder. Having more *relations,* no doubt. It's something that Lizzie would never ever admit to, especially not in front of her husband, Ralph, because she's terrified of divorce and losing this comfortable, wealthy life she has grown accustomed to. Bobby had to play along too and say he was alone on a walk, because Lizzie would never vouch for him and he knew it. And so did our killer, who knew exactly where Bobby Remy would be at the time of the murder, and that he'd never be able to prove he had an alibi. So if neither Lizzie nor Bobby is the murderer, that leaves one final person among the guests tonight."

She shifted her gaze to Zach. "Ralph Remy, you are the killer."

"What?" Connor exclaimed, though it sounded far-off somehow, in a different world from her.

"Although I'm not sure we can really call you a *killer,* seeing as your father was in on it and wanted you to do it."

"What?!" From Cara now.

"That's right. This whole thing was an elaborate plan set up by Ralph Remy, Reginald Remy, and one other person." She paused, her heart thrumming through her, right up to the point of her raised finger. "Inspector Howard Whey."

Jamie froze. He lowered his eyebrows, watching her closely.

"What?!" That one was Lauren.

"Ralph has always suspected that his brother, Bobby, murdered their mother last year. Pushed her off a cliff because she found out about his gambling again. Reginald Remy also knew, deep down, that his elder son was a murderer and had robbed him of the love of his life. But this wasn't the first time Bobby had killed someone, oh no. See, after Reginald Remy paid off Bobby's gambling debts to the loan sharks threatening his son's life, Bobby actually joined them. He was a member of the East End Streeters gang, seen dealing cocaine with them at the Garza Casino. Bobby had a serious gambling addiction to fuel, after all. A violent gang that Inspector Howard Whey and Scotland Yard have had many dealings with before. Your partner, Inspector, went undercover to try to expose the gang's drug network and was gunned down for it. But you've always known exactly who it was that shot him. It was Bobby Remy. At least two murders under his belt, and yet he would never face justice for either of them. Neither could ever be proved, and Bobby would continue living his life, free to kill again if the need arose.

"Unless someone stopped him. Fast-forward to just a

couple of months ago, when Reginald Remy found out he was dying. He knew he would never live to see justice for his poor wife, and that his elder son was a very dangerous man. So he hatched a plan with his other son, Ralph. If Bobby would never be caught for the previous two murders he'd committed, they could make damn well sure that he did go down for another murder: the murder of Reginald Remy. Reginald was going to die anyway; they might as well achieve something with his death and have Bobby locked away for life. And pay off the doctor so no one would work it out. Not only would Ralph find justice for his mother, but he could put a stop to the affair between his wife and his brother, which he knew about. Ralph and Reginald must have looked into Bobby's past and made the connection with the dead policeman, and that's when they approached Inspector Howard Whey and he came in on the plan. You, too, were desperate to see justice for your late partner, and to get this dangerous man off the streets."

"But he's not part of the game, surely?" Lauren said.

"You'd think that," Pip said, her voice running away with her. "But this information has been there all along, one of the very first things we were told. On our invitations it said that there is only one boat a day from the mainland to Joy island, leaving at twelve p.m. sharp. Today, Reginald is murdered between five-fifteen and six-thirty p.m., and then shortly after—the same evening, mind you—the inspector shows up to help us solve the murder. But how is he even here? Think about it." She leaned across the table. "It's because he was already here, had been here all day since the boat at twelve p.m. Inspector Howard Whey traveled to Joy island *before* the murder had even happened. Because he knew it was going to happen, because he was part of the plan to set Bobby Remy up for the murder of Reginald. That's why most of the clues have been mounting up to point at Bobby; the inspector has been steering the investigation."

She grabbed the ripped-up, taped-up will from the evidence pile in the center of the table. "Bobby Remy did not find and destroy this new will. Ralph and Reginald did this. We know they were in the library together alone earlier this evening. That's when they ripped it up and put it in the fireplace—and yet they didn't burn it, because they wanted it to be found. Because they were trying to establish a motive for Bobby to murder his father: money, essentially. That argument I heard last night, between Ralph and his father? They weren't talking about business plans. They were talking about *this:* their scheme to kill Reginald and set up Bobby. Remember what I overheard Ralph saying"—she double-checked against her booklet—" 'I refuse to do that, Father' and 'This scheme of yours is ridiculous and will never work' and 'won't get away with this.' Ralph was clearly getting cold feet about the whole plan, about having to stick a knife through his own father's chest. But Reginald talked him back into it.

"Look." She picked up the final clue they'd found in the pizza box. "This note from RR. Some of you thought Bobby wrote this to Lizzie, about meeting up behind Ralph's back. You might think that Bobby wrote this intentionally to give himself an alibi so he could claim he was with Lizzie at the time of the murder. But Bobby did not write this note. He is not the RR here. *This* note"—she brandished it—"was written by Reginald Remy to his son, Ralph. 'Tonight . . .'" she read from the note. "'You promised me . . . he does not deserve our sympathy.' Reginald was making sure that Ralph did not have second thoughts again. And if you don't believe me," she said, "just look at the handwriting. We have one hundred percent confirmed that Bobby wrote the other RR note to the cook about the carrot cake. Look at it: that one is printed with a different handwriting font to this one. Because they were written by two different people. And the handwriting in this note"—she waved it again—"matches the writing on our original invitations from Reginald. And in his checkbook. The truth is, Reginald organized this whole weekend to orchestrate his own murder and set up his son Bobby, with the help of Ralph—who inflicted the fatal stab wound on instruction—and the inspector, both of whom had their own scores to settle with Bobby. Robert 'Bobby' Remy is a murderer, but he's not *our* murderer. Our murder was carried out by three conspirators: Ralph Remy, Reginald Remy himself, and Inspector Howard Whey."

Pip dropped the note, watching it glide slowly to the table as she caught her breath. It landed right in front of Zach, like an arrow. He gulped.

Connor was the first to speak. "Wow," he said, clapping his hands together, staring up at her, his jaw falling open. "Just . . . wow."

"Shit, your brain is scary good," Cara laughed, the gasp real this time.

Jamie finally moved, glancing down at his master booklet, open to the final page. "That," he began, an uncertain croak in his voice. "That . . . that's wrong."

The trumpets screamed.

"What?" Pip stared at him. "What do you mean *that's wrong*?"

"Th-that's not the answer," he said, his eyes doubling back across the page. "That's not what happened. It's Bobby. Bobby's the murderer."

"Yeah, baby!" Ant shouted suddenly, making Pip flinch. He stood up, raising his arms above his head in victory. "I'm the killer, bitches!"

"No . . . ," Pip said, forcing the word out through her tightening throat. "But . . . it can't be."

"That's what it says here," Jamie said, eyebrows drawn across his eyes. "It says that Bobby murdered Reginald. Yes, you're right about Bobby murdering his mother last year, because she found out about his gambling. And Bobby was concerned his father would cut him off if he knew. This weekend he learned of the new will he'd been written out of, so he murdered his father and destroyed the new document so he'd still get his massive inheritance. And that RR note from the pizza box—like you said, Bobby wrote it to make it look like he had an alibi, like he was with Lizzie at the time of the murder. It was premeditated."

"No!" Pip said again, irritated now. "No, that can't be the solution. It's too obvious. It's too easy. It doesn't even make sense!"

"This must be absolutely killing you," Ant chuckled, "to be so epically wrong. Damn, I wish we'd been videoing you."

"No, I'm not wrong." Pip dug in her heels, feeling a flush of anger climbing up her neck, reaching for her face. "Explain the handwriting, then. How can both of the RR notes be written by Bobby if they are printed with different handwriting styles?"

"Um." Jamie flicked through his pages back and forth. "Um, no, I don't know. It doesn't say anything about that in here."

"And what about the secret clue, then? That Reginald knew he was dying of cancer? How does that figure into Bobby being the killer?"

"Um . . ." Jamie ran his finger down the page. "It says he

learned of his father's diagnosis and therefore knew that Reginald would soon be likely to draw up a new will, so he had to act quickly to secure his father's money."

"Who paid off the doctor, then? And what about you?" Pip said, her hands balling up at her sides, fingernails carving angry lines in her palms. "How does the game explain the inspector even being here if he wasn't in on the whole murder plan? There's only one boat a day at twelve p.m. You can't be here unless you knew about the murder beforehand."

Jamie's face crumpled, returning to his page. "Yeah, I, er, I don't know what to tell you, Pip. Sorry. It doesn't say anything about that in here. Just that Bobby did it."

"That's bullshit," she said.

"OK, OK." Cara tugged her back into her seat by the ends of her feather boa. "It doesn't matter, though; it's just a game."

"But it's wrong," Pip said, the fight all but leaving her, fading along with the half-moon imprints in her hands. "Bobby as the killer is too easy. It's too easy. And there are too many holes," she said, more to herself than the others. Why had she let herself get so invested? It wasn't even real.

"Well, that's OK, it's only a bit of fun," Cara said, squeezing her hand. "Besides, I guessed it, so I'm a boss."

"Yeah, and the whole game was really good," Connor said, an extra cheery edge to his voice to compensate.

"Way more interactive than I thought it would be. Thanks for setting it all up and hosting, Jame."

"Yeah, thanks, Jamie," Cara said, and Pip echoed it right after.

"That's OK, everyone," he said, removing his police hat to take a bow. "Inspector Whey, over and out."

And it had been good, right up until the end. The whole world outside this house had disappeared; it had been just Pip and her mind and a problem to solve. Exactly the way she liked it. Exactly when she was most herself.

But she'd been wrong.

Pip hated being wrong.

She ran her thumb across her closed booklet, along the logo at the bottom. With a quick, sharp movement, she made a tiny rip in the page, her small act of revenge, splitting the words *Kill Joy*.

twelve

"So how was it?" Elliot Ward asked from the front of the car. Mr. Ward filled several roles in Pip's life: Cara's dad and her history teacher. Her favorite teacher, really, but don't tell him that. She was at the Wards' house so often he had probably come to see her as a bonus daughter. She even had a *Pip* mug that lived over there.

"Yeah, really fun," Cara replied from the front. "Pip's in a semi-sulk because she guessed it wrong."

"Ah, Pip," Mr. Ward said. "Probably something wrong with the game, then, huh?" he teased, looking back quickly to smile at her and Zach sitting in the back.

"Oh my god, do not even get her started," Cara said, licking her finger to start wiping away her wrinkles.

"I preferred your theory anyway," Zach said to her across the dark backseat.

Pip gave him a closed-mouth smile. She supposed it

wasn't his fault he wasn't the murderer and that the writers at Kill Joy Games were incompetent hacks. Bobby Remy as the killer? she sniffed. It was just way too easy. OK, maybe she wasn't quite over it yet.

"So, exams all finished now," Elliot said, turning onto the main road. "Excited for your freedom, guys?"

"Oh yes," Zach said. "Got a pile of PlayStation games waiting for me."

"No shit, Sherlock" was Cara's contribution. "Though Pip isn't. Already talking about your senior capstone project, aren't ya?"

"No rest for the wicked," she quipped.

"Have you picked your topic, yet, Pip?" Elliot asked.

"Not yet," she said to the back of his head. "But I will. Soon."

They were approaching an intersection, the left turn signal blinking to go down Pip and Zach's road.

The car jolted suddenly.

Pip and Zach jerked forward against their seat belts as the car stalled.

"Dad?" Cara said, her voice edged with concern, staring across at him. He was focused on a point above her, outside the window.

"Yes, yep." He shook his head. "Sorry, kids, just thought I saw . . . someone. Got distracted. Very sorry." He turned the key in the ignition, restarting the car. "Maybe I need to come along to some of your driving lessons, Cara," he laughed as the car peeled away.

Pip turned to her window, straining to make out the dark street beyond. Mr. Ward *had* seen someone; somebody was walking past the car right now. Just another shadow until he passed under the orange glow of a street-light.

And for a second Pip saw it too, what Mr. Ward must have seen. His face. The face she knew from all the news coverage about the case, from her own fading memories. Sal Singh. Except it couldn't be; he was dead. Five years dead.

It was his younger brother, Ravi Singh. They looked so much alike from just the right angle. Pip didn't know Ravi, but like everyone else in Fairview, she knew of him.

It must have been so hard for him, living in this small town that was still so obsessed with its own small-town murder. They couldn't get away from it, no matter how many years passed; the town and those deaths came hand in hand, forever tied together. The Andie Bell case. Murdered by her boyfriend, Sal Singh. There'd never been a trial, but that was the story, what everyone believed. It was neat, done, put to bed. It's the boyfriend, it's always the boyfriend, people would say. So neat and so . . . so easy. Pip narrowed her eyes. Too easy, maybe.

She turned as far as her neck would allow, watching

Ravi as he walked away. He quickened his pace and the car drove on, splitting them apart.

Then he was gone, lost to the night.

But something else stayed behind.

"Actually," Pip said, "I think I know what I'm going to do my project on."

about the author

Holly Jackson is the author of the *New York Times* bestselling series A Good Girl's Guide to Murder, an international sensation with millions of copies sold worldwide. She is also the author of *Five Survive,* which was both an instant #1 *New York Times* bestseller and a #1 Indie bestseller. She graduated from the University of Nottingham, where she studied literary linguistics and creative writing, with a master's degree in English. She enjoys playing video games and watching true-crime documentaries so she can pretend to be a detective. She lives in London.

By the end, you'll never think the same of good girls again.

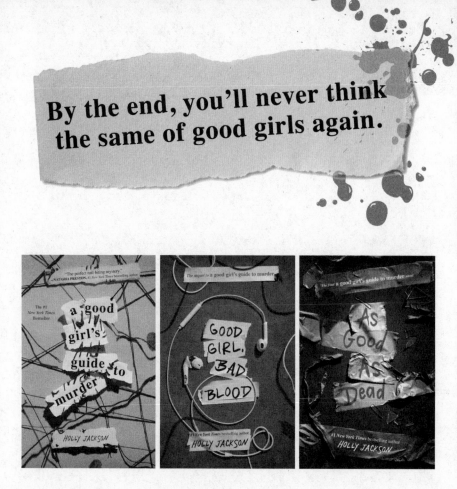

Read the entire series now!

The must-read multimillion-copy bestselling mystery series that has become a worldwide phenomenon!

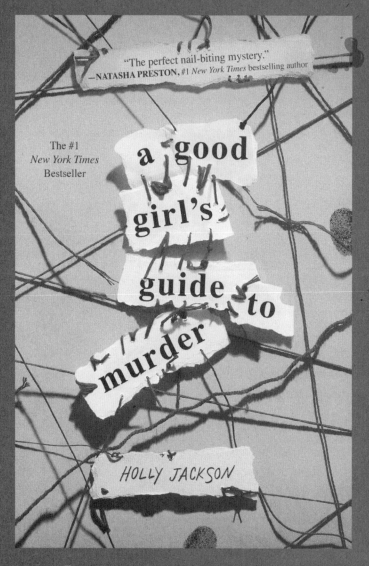

"The perfect nail-biting mystery."
—NATASHA PRESTON, #1 *New York Times* bestselling author

The #1
New York Times
Bestseller

a good girl's guide to murder

HOLLY JACKSON

Read on for the case that started it all....

part one

SENIOR CAPSTONE PROJECT PROPOSAL 2019/2020

Student number: 4169
Student's full name: Pippa Fitz-Amobi

PART A: TO BE COMPLETED BY STUDENT

The courses of study or area(s) of interest to which the topic relates:

English, Journalism, Investigative Journalism, Criminal Law

Working title of Senior Capstone Project:

"Research into the 2014 Missing Persons Investigation of
Andie Bell in Fairview, CT"

**Present the topic to be researched in the form of a statement/
question/hypothesis.**

A report on how print, televised, and social media have become
key players in police investigations, using Andie Bell as a case
study, and the implications of how the press presented Sal
Singh and his alleged guilt.

My initial resources will be:

Interview with missing persons expert, interview with a local
journalist who reported on the case, newspaper articles,
interviews with members of the community. Textbooks and
articles on police procedure, psychology, and the role of media.

SUPERVISOR'S COMMENTS:

Pippa, this is an incredibly sensitive topic, as it concerns a terrible crime that happened in our own town. Your project has been accepted only on the condition that <u>no ethical lines are crossed</u>. Please find a more focused angle for your report as you work through your research, and there is to be NO CONTACT made with either of the families involved in this case. This will be considered an ethical violation, and your project will be disqualified.

STUDENT DECLARATION:

I certify that I have read and understood the regulations as set out in the notice to students.

Signature:

PIPPA FITZ-AMOBI

Date: 7/18/19

one

Pip knew where they lived.

Everyone in Fairview knew where they lived.

Their home was like the town's own haunted house; people's footsteps quickened as they walked by, and their words strangled and died in their throats. Shrieking children would gather on their walk home from school, daring one another to run up and touch the front gate.

But it wasn't haunted by ghosts, just three sad people trying to live their lives as before. A house not haunted by flickering lights or spectral falling chairs, but by dark spray-painted letters of "Scum Family" and stone-shattered windows.

Pip had always wondered why they didn't move. Not that they had to; they hadn't done anything wrong. But she didn't know how they lived like that. How the Singhs found the strength to stay here. Here, in Fairview, under the weight of so many widened eyes, of the comments whispered just loud enough to be heard, of neighborly small talk never stretching into real talk anymore.

It was a particular cruelty that their house was so close to Fairview High School, where both Andie Bell and Sal Singh had gone, where Pip would return for her senior year in a few weeks when the late-summer sun dipped into September.

Pip stopped and rested her hand on the front gate, instantly braver than half the town's kids. Her eyes traced the path to the front door. It was possible that this was a very bad idea; she had considered that.

Pausing for just a second, Pip held her breath, then pushed the creaking gate and crossed the yard. She stopped at the door and knocked three times. Her reflection stared back at her: the long dark hair sun-bleached a lighter brown at the tips, the pale white skin despite a week just spent in the Caribbean, the sharp muddy-green eyes braced for impact.

The door opened with the clatter of a falling chain and clicking locks.

"H-hello?" he said, holding the door half open, with his hand folded over the side. Pip blinked to break her stare, but she couldn't help it. He looked so much like Sal: the Sal she knew from all those television reports and newspaper pictures. The Sal now fading from her memory. Ravi had his brother's messy black side-swept hair, thick arched eyebrows, and oaken-hued skin.

"Hello?" he said again.

"Um . . ." Pip faltered. He'd grown even taller since she last saw him. She'd never been this close before, but now that she was, she saw he had a dimple in his chin, just like hers. "Um, sorry, hi." She did an awkward half wave that she immediately regretted.

"Hi?"

"Hi, Ravi," she said. "I . . . You don't know me. . . . I'm Pippa Fitz-Amobi. I was a few years below you at school before you left."

"OK . . ."

"I was just wondering if I could borrow a second of your time? Well, not *only* a second, we're already way past that. . . . Maybe like a few sequential seconds, if you can spare them?"

Oh god, this was what happened when she was nervous: words spewed out, unchecked and overexplained, until someone stopped her.

Ravi looked confused.

"Sorry," Pip said, recovering. "I mean, I'm doing my senior capstone project at school and—"

"What's a capstone project?"

"It's kind of like a senior thesis you work on independently, alongside normal classes. You can pick any topic you want, and I was wondering if you'd be willing to be interviewed for mine."

"What's it about?" His dark eyebrows hugged closer to his eyes.

"Um . . . it's about what happened five years ago."

Ravi exhaled loudly, his lip curling with what looked like anger.

"Why?" he said.

"Because I don't think your brother did it—and I'm going to try to prove it."

PIPPA FITZ-AMOBI
7/30/19
CAPSTONE PROJECT LOG—ENTRY 1

Our capstone project logs are supposed to be for recording any obstacles we face in our research; our progress; and the aims of our final reports. Mine will have to be a little different: I'm going to record all my research here, both relevant and irrelevant, because I don't really know what my final report will be yet or what will end up being important. I will just have to wait and see where I'm at after all my investigating and what essay I can bring together.

I'm hoping it will *not* be the topic I proposed to Mrs. Morgan. I'm hoping it will be the truth. What really happened to Andie Bell on April 18, 2014? And if—as my instincts tell me—Salil "Sal" Singh is not guilty, then who killed her?

I don't think I'll actually solve the case and figure out who murdered Andie. I'm not deluded. But I'm hoping my findings might lead to reasonable doubt about Sal's guilt, and suggest that the police were mistaken in closing the case without digging further.

The first stage in this project is to research what happened to Andrea Bell—known to everyone as Andie—and the circumstances surrounding her disappearance.

From the first national online news outlet to report on the event:

> *Andrea Bell, seventeen, was reported missing from her home in Fairview, Connecticut, last Friday.*
> *She left home in her car—a white Honda Civic—with her cell phone, but did not take any clothes with her. Police say her disappearance is "completely out of character."*

Police began searching the woodland near the family home this past weekend.

Andrea, known as Andie, is described as white, five feet six inches tall, with long blond hair and blue eyes. It is thought that she was wearing dark jeans and a blue cropped sweater on the night she went missing.[1]

Other sources had more details as to when Andie was last seen alive, and the time frame in which she is believed to have been abducted.

Andie Bell was "last seen alive by her younger sister, Becca, around 10:30 p.m. on April 18, 2014."[2]

This was corroborated by the police in a press conference on Tuesday, April 22: "Footage taken from a security camera outside the bank on Fairview's Main Street confirms that Andie's car was seen driving away from her home at about 10:40 p.m."[3]

According to her parents, Jason and Dawn Bell, Andie was "supposed to pick (them) up from a dinner party at 12:45 a.m." When Andie didn't show up or answer any of their phone calls, they started reaching out to her friends to see if anyone knew of her whereabouts. Jason Bell "called the police to report his daughter missing at 3:00 a.m. Saturday morning."[4]

So whatever happened to Andie Bell that night happened between 10:40 p.m. and 12:45 a.m.

Here seems like a good place to type up the transcript from my interview with Angela Johnson.

---

1 www.ustn.com/news/2014/04/21/local-teen-missing, 4/21/14

2 www.fairfieldctnews.com/fairview/crime-4839, 4/24/14

3 www.ustn.com/news/2014/04/22/missing-schoolgirl-698834, 4/22/14

4 Forbes, Stanley, 2014, "The Real Story of Andie Bell's Killer," *Fairview Mail*, 4/29/14, pp. 1–4.

TRANSCRIPT OF INTERVIEW WITH ANGELA JOHNSON
FROM THE MISSING PERSONS BUREAU

ANGELA: Hello.

PIP: Hi, is this Angela Johnson?

ANGELA: Speaking, yep. Is this Pippa?

PIP: Yes, thanks so much for replying to my email. Do you mind if I record this interview for my project?

ANGELA: Yeah, that's fine. I'm sorry, I've only got about ten minutes. So what do you want to know about missing persons?

PIP: Well, I was wondering if you could talk me through what happens when someone is reported missing? What's the process and the first steps taken by the police?

ANGELA: When someone is reported missing, the police will try to get as much detail as possible so they can identify the potential risk to the missing person, and an appropriate police response can be made. They'll ask for name, age, description, the clothes they were last seen wearing, the circumstances of their disappearance, if going missing is out of character for this person, details of any vehicle involved. Using this information, the police will determine whether this is an at-risk missing persons case.

PIP: And what circumstances would make it an at-risk case?

ANGELA: If they are vulnerable because of their age or a disability, or if the behavior is out of character, which indicates they could have been exposed to harm.

PIP: Um, so, if the missing person is seventeen years old and it is deemed out of character for her to go missing, would that be considered an at-risk case?

ANGELA: Absolutely, when a minor is involved.

PIP: So how would the police respond?

ANGELA: Well, there would be immediate deployment of police officers to the location the person is missing from. The officers will get further information about the missing person, such as details of their friends or partners; any health conditions; financial information, in case they try to withdraw money. Police will also need recent photographs and might take DNA samples, in case they're needed in subsequent forensic examinations. And, with consent of the homeowners, the location would be searched thoroughly to see if the missing person is concealed or hiding there and to establish whether there are any further evidential leads.

PIP: So immediately the police are looking for any clues or suggestions that the missing person has been the victim of a crime?

ANGELA: Absolutely. If the circumstances of the disappearance are suspicious, officers are instructed to document evidence early on, as though they were investigating a murder. Of course, only a very small percentage of missing persons cases turn into homicide cases.

PIP: And what happens if nothing significant turns up after the initial home search?

ANGELA: They'll expand the search to the immediate area. They'll question friends, neighbors, anyone who might have relevant information. If it is a teenager who's missing, we can't assume the reporting parent knows all of their child's friends and acquaintances. Peers are good points of contact to establish other important leads—you know, any secret boyfriends, that sort of thing. And a press strategy is usually discussed because appeals for information in the media can be very useful in these situations.

PIP: So if it's a seventeen-year-old girl who's gone missing, the police would contact her friends and boyfriend early on?

ANGELA: Yes, of course. Inquiries will be made, because if the missing person has run away, they are likely to be hiding out with someone close to them.

PIP: And at what point in a missing persons case do police assume they are looking for a body?

ANGELA: Well, timewise, it's not— Oh, Pippa, I have to go. Sorry, I've been called into my meeting.

PIP: Oh, OK, thanks so much for taking the time to talk to me.

ANGELA: And if you have more questions, just shoot me an email and I'll get to it when I can.

PIP: Will do, thanks again.

I found these statistics:

80% of missing people are found in the first twenty-four hours. 97% are found in the first week, and 99% of cases are resolved in the first year.

That leaves just 1%. 1% of people who disappear are never found. And just 0.25% of all missing persons cases have a fatal outcome.[5] So where does this leave Andie Bell? Floating incessantly somewhere between 1% and 0.25%.

Even though Andie has never been found and her body never recovered, most people accept that she is dead. And why is that?

Sal Singh is why.

---

5 www.missingpersonstats.com

two

Pip's hands hovered over the keyboard as she strained to listen to the commotion downstairs. A crash, heavy footsteps, skidding claws, and unrestrained boyish giggles.

"Josh! Why is the dog wearing my shirt!" Pip's dad shouted, the sound floating upstairs.

Pip snort-laughed as she clicked to save her capstone project log and closed her laptop. It was never quiet once her dad returned from work.

Downstairs, Pip found Josh running from room to room— kitchen to hallway to living room—on repeat. Cackling as he went.

Close behind was Barney, the golden retriever, wearing her dad's loudest shirt, the blindingly green patterned one he'd bought during their last trip to Nigeria. The dog skidded elatedly across the polished oak in the hall, excitement whistling through his teeth.

Bringing up the rear was Pip's dad in his gray Hugo Boss three-piece suit, all six and a half feet of him charging after the dog and the boy, laughing in wild bursts.

"Oh my god, I was trying to do homework," Pip said, restraining a smile as she jumped back to avoid being mowed down. Barney stopped for a moment to headbutt her shin and then

scampered off to jump on Victor and Josh as they collapsed together on the sofa.

"Hello, pickle," her dad said, patting the couch beside him.

"Hi, Dad. You were so quiet I didn't even know you were home."

"My Pipsicle, you are too clever to recycle a joke."

She sat down beside them. Josh started excavating his right
nostril, and Pip's dad batted his hand away. "How were your days,
then?" her dad asked, setting Josh off on a graphic spiel about the
soccer games he'd played earlier.

Pip zoned out; she'd already heard it all in the car when she
picked Josh up from practice. She'd only been half listening, distracted by the way the replacement coach had stared at her, uncertain, when she'd pointed out which of the nine-year-olds was
hers and said: "I'm Josh's sister."

She should have been used to it by now, the lingering looks
while people tried to work out the logistics of her family. Victor,
the tall Nigerian man, was evidently her stepfather; and Josh, her
half brother. But Pip didn't like those words, those cold technical-
ities. The people you love weren't calculated, subtracted, or held
at arm's length across a decimal point. Victor was her dad, who'd
raised her since she was four years old, and Josh was her annoying
little brother.

Her "real" father, the man who lent the Fitz to her name, died in
a car accident when she was ten months old. And though Pip nodded and smiled when her mom would ask whether she remembered the way her father hummed while he brushed his teeth or
how he'd laughed when Pip's second spoken word was "poo," she
didn't remember him. But sometimes remembering isn't for yourself; sometimes you do it just to make someone else smile.

"And how's the project going, Pip?" Her dad turned to her as he
unbuttoned the shirt from the dog.

"It's OK," she said. "I'm just researching at the moment. I did go to see Ravi Singh this morning, though."

"Oh, and . . . ?"

"He was busy, but he said I could go back on Friday."

"I wouldn't," Josh said in a cautionary tone.

"That's because you're a judgmental prepubescent boy who still thinks little people live inside traffic lights." Pip looked at him. "The Singhs haven't done anything wrong."

Victor stepped in. "Josh, try to imagine if everyone judged you because of something your sister had done."

"All Pip ever does is homework."

She swung a cushion into Josh's face, and her dad held the boy's arms down as he squirmed to retaliate, tickling his ribs.

As Pip watched them play-fighting, she couldn't help but wonder whether the Singhs ever laughed like that anymore. Or the Bells.

Maybe laughter was one of the very first things you lost after something like that.

PIPPA FITZ-AMOBI
7/31/19
CAPSTONE PROJECT LOG—ENTRY 2

What happened next in the Andie Bell case is hard to piece together from the newspaper reports, so I have to fill in the gaps with guesswork and rumors until the picture becomes clearer. Hopefully, interviews with Ravi and Naomi—who was one of Sal's best friends—will help.

According to what Angela said, the police would have asked for details about Andie's friends early on, presumably after taking statements from the Bell family.

After some serious social media stalking, it looks like Andie's best friends were two girls named Chloe Burch and Emma Hutton.

 Emma Hutton, Sal Singh and 97 others
View 6 more comments

Emma Hutton Oh my god Andie, stop being so gorge.
Like · Reply · 5y

Chloe Burch I wish I didn't have to be in pics with you. Give me your face
Like · Reply · 5y

Andie Bell No ;)
Like · Reply · 5y

Emma Hutton Andie, let's take a nice one at the next calamity? Need new prof pic :)
Like · Reply · 5y

Write a comment . . .

This post was from almost two weeks before Andie disappeared. It looks like neither Chloe nor Emma lives in Fairview anymore, but I'll message them to see if they'll do a phone interview.

Chloe and Emma did a lot on that first weekend (April 19 and 20) to help spread the Connecticut State Police's Twitter campaign: #FindAndie. I don't think it's too big of a leap to assume that the police contacted Chloe and Emma either on the Friday night Andie went missing or the next morning. What they said to the police, I don't know. Hopefully, I can find out.

We do know that police spoke to Andie's boyfriend at the time. His name was Sal Singh, and he was attending his senior year at Fairview High along with Andie.

At some point on Saturday, April 19, the police contacted him:

> *"Detective Richard Hawkins confirmed that officers had questioned Salil Singh as to his whereabouts the previous night, particularly the period of time during which it is believed Andie went missing."*[6]

Friday night, Sal had been hanging out at his friend Max Hastings's house. He was with his four best friends: Naomi Ward, Jake Lawrence, Millie Simpson, and Max.

Again, I need to check this with Naomi next week, but I think Sal told the police that he left Max's around 12:15 a.m. He walked home, and his father (Mohan Singh) confirmed that "Sal returned home at approximately 12:50 a.m."[7] [Note: the distance between Max's house (Courtland) and Sal's (Grove Place) takes about thirty minutes to walk.]

The police confirmed Sal's alibi with his four friends over that weekend.

---

6 www.ustn.com/news/2014/05/03/fairview-murder, 5/3/14

7 www.ustn.com/news/2014/05/03/fairview-murder, 5/3/14

Missing posters went up. House-to-house inquiries started on the Sunday.[8]

On the Monday one hundred volunteers helped the police carry out searches in the local woodland. I've seen the news footage; a whole ant line of people in the trees, calling her name. Later in the day forensic teams were spotted going into the Bell residence.[9]

And on the Tuesday everything changed. I think chronologically is the best way to consider the events of that day, and those that followed, even though we, as a town, learned the details out of order and jumbled:

Midmorning: Naomi Ward, Max Hastings, Jake Lawrence, and Millie Simpson contacted the police from school and confessed to providing false information. They said that Sal had asked them to lie and that he actually left Max's house around 10:30 p.m. on the night Andie disappeared, not 12:15 a.m.

I don't know for sure what the correct police procedure would have been, but I'm guessing at that point, Sal became the number one suspect.

But no one could find him: Sal wasn't at school and he wasn't at home. He wasn't answering his phone. It later came out, however, that Sal had sent a text to his father that Tuesday morning, though he was ignoring all other calls. The press would refer to this as a "confession text."[10]

Tuesday evening, one of the police teams searching for Andie found a body in the woods.

It was Sal.

He had killed himself.

The press never reported the method by which Sal committed

8 Forbes, Stanley, "Local Girl Still Missing," *Fairview Mail*, 4/21/14, pp. 1–2.

9 www.ustn.com/news/2014/04/21/fairview-missing-girl, 4/21/14

10 www.ustn.com/news/2014/05/03/fairview-murder, 5/3/14

suicide, but by the power of small-town rumor, I knew (as did every other student at Fairview at the time).

Sal walked into the woods near his home, took a huge dose of sleeping pills, and placed a plastic bag over his head, securing it with an elastic band around his neck. He suffocated while unconscious.

At the police press conference that night, there was no mention of Sal. The police only revealed the information about security footage placing Andie driving away from her home at 10:40 p.m.[11]

On Wednesday Andie's car was found parked on a small residential road (Monroe).

It wasn't until the following Monday that a police spokeswoman revealed the following:

> "As a result of recent intelligence and forensic information, we have strong reason to suspect that a young man named Salil Singh, aged eighteen, was involved in Andie's abduction and murder. The evidence would have been sufficient to arrest and charge the suspect had he not died before proceedings could be initiated. Police are not looking for anyone else in relation to Andie's disappearance at this time, but our search for Andie will continue unabated. Our thoughts go out to the Bell family, and our deepest sympathies for the devastation this update has caused them."

Their sufficient evidence:

- They found Andie's phone on Sal's body.
- Forensic tests found traces of Andie's blood under the fingernails of his right middle and index fingers.

11 www.ustn.com/news/2014/04/22/fairview-girl-still-missing, 4/22/14

- Andie's blood was discovered in the trunk of her abandoned car.
- Sal's fingerprints were found around the dashboard and steering wheel, alongside prints from Andie and the rest of the Bell family.[12]

The evidence, they said, would have been enough to charge Sal. But he was dead, so there was no trial and no conviction. No defense either.

In the following weeks there were more searches of the woodland areas in and around Fairview. Searches using cadaver dogs. Police divers in the river. Andie's body was never found. The Andie Bell missing persons case was administratively closed in the middle of June 2014.[13]

Eighteen months later a court order was filed and Andie Bell was declared dead in absentia, based on the circumstances surrounding her disappearance. Andie Bell's death certificate was issued.[14] Despite her body never having been located, she has now been legally declared dead.

After the ruling the district attorney said: "The case against Salil Singh would have been based on circumstantial and forensic evidence. It is not for me to state whether or not Salil Singh killed Andie Bell; that would have been a jury's job to decide."[15]

And even though there has never been a trial, no conviction by a jury; even though Sal never had the chance to defend himself, he is guilty. Not in the legal sense, but in all the other ways that truly matter.

---

12 www.ustn.com/news/2014/05/07/fairview-andie-bell-murder, 5/7/14
13 www.ustn.com/news/2014/06/15/andie-bell-case-closed, 6/15/14
14 www.thenewsroom.com/AndieBellInquest/report57743, 1/12/16
15 www.ustn.com/news/2016/01/15/fairview-murder-DA-statement, 1/15/16

When you ask people in town what happened to Andie Bell, they'll tell you without hesitation: "She was murdered by Salil Singh." No "allegedly," no "might have," no "probably," no "most likely."

He did it, they say. Sal Singh killed Andie.

But I'm just not so sure.

three

It was an emergency, the text said. An SOS emergency. Pip knew immediately that that could only mean one thing.

She grabbed her car keys, yelled goodbye to her mom and Josh, and rushed out the front door.

She stopped by the store on her way to buy a king-size chocolate bar to help mend Lauren's king-size broken heart.

When she pulled up outside the Gibsons' house, she saw that Cara had had the exact same idea. Except Cara's post-breakup first-aid kit was more extensive than Pip's; she had also brought a box of tissues, chips and dip, and a rainbow array of face mask packets.

"Ready for this?" Pip asked Cara, hip-bumping her in greeting.

"Yep, well prepared for the tears." She held up the tissues, the corner of the box catching the ends of her curly ash-brown hair.

Pip pressed the doorbell, and both of them winced at the mechanical song.

Lauren's mom answered the door.

"Oh, the cavalry is here." She smiled. "She's upstairs in her room."

They found Lauren fully submerged in a duvet fort on the bed, the only sign of her existence a splay of ginger hair poking out from the bottom. It took a full minute of coaxing and chocolate bait to get her to surface.

"First," Cara said, prying Lauren's phone from her fingers, nails bitten to the quick, "you're banned from looking at this for the next twenty-four hours."

"He did it by text!" Lauren wailed, blowing her nose and shooting an entire swamp into the tissue.

"Boys are dicks," Cara said, putting her arm around Lauren and resting her sharp chin on her shoulder. "You could do so much better than him."

"Yeah." Pip broke Lauren off another line of chocolate. "Besides, Tom always said 'pacifically' when he meant 'specifically.'"

Cara pointed eagerly at Pip in agreement. "Massive red flag."

"I *pacifically* think you're better off without him," said Pip.

"I *atlantically* think so too," added Cara.

Lauren gave a wet snort of laughter, and Cara winked at Pip; an unspoken victory.

"Thanks for coming, guys," Lauren said tearfully, her pale eyes swollen and puffy. "I didn't know if you would. I've probably neglected you for half a year to hang out with Tom. And now I'll be third-wheeling two best friends."

"That's crap," Cara said. "We're all best friends."

"Yeah." Pip nodded. "Us, and those three mediocre boys we allow to bask in our delightful company."

Cara and Lauren laughed. The boys—Ant, Zach, and Connor—were all currently away during the summer break.

But of her friends, Pip had known Cara the longest, and yes, they were closest. An unsaid thing. They'd been inseparable ever since six-year-old Cara had hugged a tiny, friendless Pip and asked, "Do you like bunnies too?"

They were each other's crutch to lean on when life got too much to carry alone. Pip, though only ten at the time, had helped Cara through her mom's diagnosis and death. And Pip had been her constant two years ago when Cara came out, ready with a steady smile and phone calls into the early hours. Cara's wasn't the face of a best friend; it was the face of a sister.

By extension, Cara's family was Pip's second. Mr. Ward, in addition to being her history teacher, was her tertiary father figure, behind her stepdad and the ghost of her first father. Pip was at the Ward house so often she had her own mug with her name on it and pair of slippers to match Cara's and her older sister, Naomi's.

"OK." Cara lunged for the TV remote. "Rom-coms or films where boys get violently murdered?"

It took roughly one and a half terrible films from the Netflix backlog for Lauren to wade through denial and extend a cautionary toe toward acceptance.

"I should get a haircut," she said. "That's what you're supposed to do."

"I've always said you'd look good with short hair," said Cara.

"And do you think I should get my nose pierced?"

"Ooh, yeah." Cara nodded.

"I don't see the logic in putting a nose hole in your nose hole," said Pip.

"Another Pip quote for the books." Cara feigned writing it down in midair. "What was the one that got me the other day?"

"The sausage one." Pip sighed.

"Oh yeah," Cara snorted. "So, Laur, I was asking Pip which pajamas she wanted to wear, and she just casually says, 'It's sausage to me.' And didn't realize why that was a weird response."

"It's not that weird," said Pip. "My grandparents from my first dad are German. 'It's sausage to me' is a German saying; just means 'I don't care.'"

"Or you've got a sausage fixation." Lauren laughed.

"Says the daughter of a porn star," Pip quipped.

"Oh my god, how many times? He only did one nude photo-shoot in the eighties, that's it."

"So, on to boys from this decade," Cara said, prodding Pip on the shoulder. "Did you go see Ravi Singh yet?"

"Questionable segue. But yes, and I'm going back to interview him tomorrow."

"I can't believe you've already started your capstone project," Lauren said with a dying-swan dive back onto the bed. "I want to change mine already; famines are depressing."

"I imagine you want to interview Naomi sometime soon." Cara looked pointedly at Pip.

"Yeah. . . . Can you warn her I might be stopping by next week?"

"Sure," Cara said, then hesitated. "She'll agree to it and everything, but can you go easy on her? She still gets really upset about it sometimes. I mean, he was one of her best friends. Actually, probably her *best* friend."

"Yeah, of course," Pip said. "What do you think I'm going to do? Pin her down and beat responses out of her?"

"Is that your tactic for Ravi tomorrow?"

"Ha."

Lauren sat up then, with a snot-sucking sniff so loud it made Cara visibly flinch.

"Are you going to his house, then?" she asked.

"Yeah."

"But . . . what are people going to think if they see you going into Ravi Singh's house?"

"It's sausage to me."

I'm biased; I know I am. For reasons I don't even know how to explain to myself, I want Sal Singh to be innocent. Reasons carried with me since I was twelve years old, inconsistencies that have nagged at me these past five years.

But if I'm actually going to solve anything, I have to be aware of confirmation bias. So I thought it would be a good idea to interview someone who is utterly convinced of Sal's guilt.

Stanley Forbes, a journalist at the *Fairview Mail*, just responded to my email, saying I could call any time today. He covered a lot of the Andie Bell case in the local press and was even present at the court hearing when she was declared dead a year and a half later. To be honest I think he's a poor journalist, and I'm pretty sure the Singhs could sue him for defamation and libel about a dozen times over. I'll type up the transcript here right after.

TRANSCRIPT OF INTERVIEW WITH STANLEY FORBES
FROM THE *FAIRVIEW MAIL* NEWSPAPER

PIP: Hi, Stanley. This is Pippa; we were emailing earlier.

STANLEY: Yep, yeah, I know. You wanted to pick my brain about the Andie Bell/Salil Singh case, right?

PIP: Yes, that's right. Do you mind if I record our conversation?

STANLEY: Sure, shoot.

PIP: OK, thanks. Um, so first, you attended the court hearing that established Andie as legally dead, correct?

STANLEY: Sure did.

PIP: Since the national press didn't elaborate much further than reporting the verdict, I was wondering if you could tell me what kind of evidence was presented?

STANLEY: Uh, so the main investigator on Andie's case outlined the details of her disappearance—the times and so on. And then he moved on to the evidence that linked Salil to her murder. They made a big deal about the blood in the trunk of her car; they said this suggested that she was murdered and her body was put in the trunk to be transported somewhere else. They said something like "It seems clear that Andie was the victim of a sexually motivated murder, and considerable efforts were made to dispose of her body."

PIP: And did Detective Richard Hawkins or any other officer provide a timeline of what they believed were the events of that night and how Sal allegedly killed her?

STANLEY: Yeah, I kinda remember that. Andie left home in her car, and at some point on Salil's walk home, he intercepted her. With either him or her driving, he took her to a secluded place and murdered her. He put her in the trunk and then drove somewhere to hide or dispose of her body. Mind you, well enough that it hasn't been found in five years; must have been a pretty big hole. And then he ditched the car on that road where it was found—Monroe, I think—and he walked home.

PIP: So because of the blood in the trunk, the police believed that Andie was killed somewhere and then hidden in a different location?

STANLEY: Yep.

PIP: OK. In a lot of your articles about the case, you refer to Sal as a "killer," a "murderer," and even a "monster." You are aware that without a conviction, you are supposed to use the word "allegedly" when reporting crime stories.

STANLEY: Not sure I need a child to tell me how to do my job. Anyway, it's obvious that he did it, and everyone knows it. He killed her, and the guilt drove him to suicide.

PIP: And why are you so convinced Sal's guilty?

STANLEY: Almost too many things to list. Evidence aside, he was the boyfriend, right? And it's always the boyfriend or the ex-boyfriend. Not only that, Salil was Indian.

PIP: Well . . . he was actually born and raised in the United States, though it is notable you refer to him as Indian in all of your articles.

STANLEY: Well, same thing. He was of Indian heritage.

PIP: And why is that relevant?

STANLEY: I'm not like an expert or anything, but they have different ways of life from us, don't they? They don't treat women quite like we do. So I'm guessing maybe Andie decided she didn't want to be with him or something, and he killed her in a rage because, in his eyes, she belonged to him.

PIP: Wow . . . I . . . Honestly, Stanley, I'm pretty surprised you still have a job.

STANLEY: That's 'cause everyone knows what I'm saying is true.

PIP: I don't agree. And I think it's irresponsible to publicly call someone a murderer without using "allegedly" when there's been no conviction. Or, even worse, calling Sal a monster. It's interesting to compare your reporting about Sal to your recent articles on the Stratford Strangler. He murdered five people and pleaded guilty, yet in your headline you referred to him as a "lovesick young man." Is that because *he's* white?

STANLEY: That's got nothing to do with Salil's case; I just call it how it is. You need to relax. He's dead. Why does it matter if people call him a murderer? It can't hurt him.

PIP: Because his family isn't dead.

STANLEY: Look, this is a waste of my time. You really think he's innocent? Against the expertise of senior officers?

PIP: I just think there are certain gaps in the case against Sal, that's all.

STANLEY: Yeah, maybe if the kid hadn't offed himself before getting arrested, we would have been able to fill the gaps.

PIP: That was insensitive.

STANLEY: Well, it was insensitive of him to kill his girlfriend.

PIP: Allegedly!

STANLEY: You want more proof that that kid was a killer, fangirl? We weren't allowed to print it, but my source in the police said they found a death-threat note in Andie's school locker. He threatened her, and then he did it. Do you really still think he's innocent?

PIP: Maybe he is. And you're a racist, intolerant hack who— (Stanley hangs up the phone.)

Yeah, so I don't think Stanley and I are going to be best friends. But he's provided two pieces of information I didn't have before. First: police believe Andie was killed somewhere before being put in the trunk of her car and driven to a second location to be disposed of. Second: this "death threat." I haven't seen a death threat mentioned in any articles or police statements. Maybe the police didn't think it was relevant. Or maybe they couldn't prove it was linked to Sal. Or maybe Stanley made it up. In any case, it's worth remembering when I interview Andie's friends later on.

So now that I (sort of) know what the police's version of events are for that night, and what the prosecution's case might have looked like, it's time for a *murder map*.

I had to make a couple of assumptions when creating it. The first is that there are several ways to walk from Max's to Sal's; I picked the one that heads back through Main Street, because Google said it was the quickest and I'm presuming most people prefer to walk on well-lit streets at night.

It also provides a good intercept point somewhere along Weevil Road, where Andie possibly pulled over and Sal got in the car. There are some quiet residential roads and a farm on Weevil Road. These secluded places—circled—could potentially be the site of the murder (according to the police's version of events).

I didn't bother guessing where Andie's body was disposed because, like the rest of the world, I have no clue where that is. But given that it takes about eighteen minutes to walk from where the car was dumped on Monroe back to Sal's house on Grove Place, I have to presume he'd have been back in the vicinity of Weevil Road around 12:20 a.m. If the Andie-and-Sal intercept happened around 10:45 p.m., this would have given Sal one hour and thirty-five minutes to murder her and hide her body. I mean, timewise, that seems perfectly reasonable to me. It's possible.

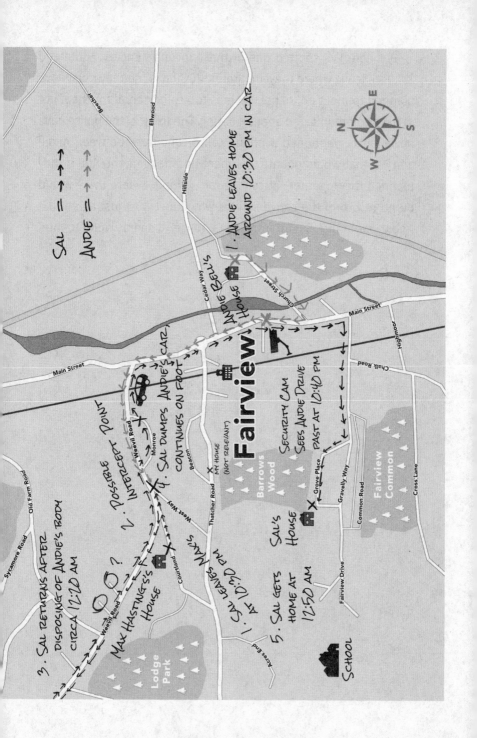

But here I've spotted one of those inconsistencies. Andie and Sal both leave where they are around 10:30 p.m., so they must have planned to meet up, right? It seems too coincidental for them not to have communicated about meeting. The thing is, the police have never once mentioned a phone call or any texts between Andie and Sal that would equate to a meet-up arrangement. And if they planned this together—at school, for example, where there would be no record of the conversation—why didn't they just agree that Andie would pick Sal up from Max's house? It seems weird to me.

Eight hours.
Six friends.
Five survive.

FIVE SURVIVE

Gear up for the latest YA thriller
from Holly Jackson about a road
trip that turns deadly!

10:00 P.M.

ONE

Here and not. Red and black. One moment there, another gone. Her face in the glass. Disappearing in the light of oncoming headlights, reappearing in the dark of outside. Gone again. The window kept her face for its own. Good, it could keep it. Back, the window didn't want it either.

Red's reflection stared through her, but the glass and the darkness didn't get her quite right, blurring the details. The main features were there: the too-pale glow of her skin and the wide-set dark blue eyes that weren't hers alone. *You look so much alike,* she used to hear, more than she cared to. Now she didn't care to hear it at all, even think it. So, she looked away from her face, their face, ignoring them both. But it was harder to ignore something when you were trying.

Red shifted her gaze, looking instead at the cars in the lane beside and below. Something wasn't right; the cars seemed too small from up here at her window, but Red didn't feel any bigger. She watched a blue sedan edging forward to pass, and she helped it along with her eyes, pushing them ahead. There you go, bud. Ahead of this thirty-one-foot-long metal can, speeding down the highway. Which was strange when you thought about it; that you traveled *down* a highway when *high* was right there in the name.

"Red?" The voice opposite interrupted her thoughts of lowways and highways. Maddy was looking at her through the dimmed inside lights, skin screwed up around her sandy-brown eyes. She gave a small kick under the table, jabbing Red in the shin. "Did you just forget we were in the middle of playing a game?"

"No," Red said, but yes, yes she had. What had they been playing again?

"Twenty Questions," Maddy said, reading Red's mind. Well, they had known each other all their lives; Red had only gotten a seven-month head start and she hadn't done a lot with it. Maybe Maddy had learned to read her mind in all that time, more than seventeen years. Red really hoped not. There were things in there no one else could ever see. No one. Not even Maddy. Especially not Maddy.

"Yeah, I know," Red said, her eyes wandering to the other side of the RV, to the outside door and the sofa bed—currently sofa—where she and Maddy would sleep tonight. Red couldn't remember; which side of the bed did Maddy like again? Because she couldn't sleep if she wasn't on the left side, and just as she was trying to read Maddy's mind back about that, her eyes caught on a green sign outside in the night, flying over the windshield.

"That sign says Rockingham, aren't we getting off this road soon?" Red said, not loud enough for anyone at the very front of the RV to hear, where it would have been more use. She was probably wrong, anyway, best to say nothing. They'd been driving on this same road for the past hour, I-73 becoming I-74 and then US 220 without much fanfare.

"Red Kenny, focus." Maddy snapped her fingers, a hint of a smile on her face. It never creased, though, Maddy's face, not even with the widest of smiles. Skin like cream, soft and clearer than it had any business being. It made the freckles on Red's face stand out even more, side by side in photos. Literally side by side; they were almost the exact same height, down to the highest-standing hair, though Red's was dark blond where Maddy's was more light brown, a shade or two separating them. Red always had hers tied back, loose bangs at the front that she'd cut herself with the kitchen scissors. Maddy's was untied and neat, the ends soft in a way Red's never were. "I'm the one asking questions, you're the one with the person, place or thing," Maddy prompted.

Red nodded slowly. Well, even if Maddy also liked to sleep on the left, at least they weren't on the bunks.

"I've asked seven questions already," Maddy said.

"Great." Red couldn't remember her person, place or thing. But really, they'd been driving all day, setting off from home around twelve hours ago, hadn't they played enough road trip games? Red couldn't wait for this to be over so she could finally sleep, whether left side or right. Just get through it. They were supposed to arrive at Gulf Shores around this time tomorrow, meet up with the rest of their friends, that was the plan.

Maddy cleared her throat.

"And what answers did I give, remind me?" Red said.

Maddy breathed out, an almost sigh or an almost laugh, hard to tell. "It was a person, a woman, not a fictional character," she said, counting them off on her fingers. "Someone I would know, but not Kim Kardashian or you."

Red looked up, searching the empty corners of her mind for the memory. "No, sorry," she said, "it's gone."

"Okay, we'll start again," Maddy said, but just then, Simon stumbled out of the small bathroom, saving Red from more Organized Fun™. The door bounced back into him as the RV sped up.

"Simon Yoo, have you been in there this whole time?" Maddy asked, disgusted. "We've played two whole rounds."

Simon pushed his black, loosely waved hair away from his face and held an unsteady finger to his lips, saying, "Shh, a lady never tells."

"Shut the door, then, jeez."

He did, but with his foot, to make some point or other, almost overbalancing as they hurtled along the highway, changing lanes to pass. Wasn't their exit soon? Maybe Red should say something, but now she was watching as Simon waded forward, leaning on the tiny kitchen counter behind her. In one awkward motion, he slid onto the booth beside her, knocking his knees on the table.

Red studied him: his pupils were sitting too large in his dark, round eyes, and there was an incriminating wet patch on the front of his teal-colored Eagles shirt.

"You're drunk already," she said, almost impressed. "I thought you'd only had like three beers."

Simon moved close to whisper in her ear, and Red could smell the sharp metallic tang on his breath. She couldn't miss it; that was how she knew when her dad was lying to her, *No I didn't drink today, Red, I promise.* "Shh," Simon said, "Oliver brought tequila."

"And you just helped yourself?" Maddy asked, overhearing.

In answer, Simon balled both his fists and held them in the air, yelling: "Spring break, baby!"

Red laughed. And anyway, if she just asked, maybe Maddy wouldn't mind sleeping on the right tonight, or for the rest of the week. She could just ask.

"Oliver doesn't like people touching his things," Maddy said quietly, glancing over her shoulder at her brother, sitting just a few feet behind her in the front passenger seat, fiddling with the radio as he chatted to Reyna in the driver's seat. Arthur was standing just behind

Oliver and Reyna, now shooting a closed-mouth smile as he caught Red's eye. Or maybe it was actually Simon he was smiling at.

"Hey, it's my RV, I have a claim to anything in it," Simon hiccupped.

"Your uncle's RV." Maddy felt the need to correct him.

"Weren't you supposed to have a driving shift today too?" Red asked him. The plan was to share the drive equally among the six of them. She had taken the first two-hour shift, to get it out of the way, driving them out of Philly and down I-95 until they stopped for lunch. Arthur had sat with her the whole time, calmly directing her, as though he could tell when she was zoning in and out, or when she was panicking about the size of the RV and how small everything looked from up here. Mind readers everywhere, clearly. But she'd only known Arthur six or seven months; that wasn't fair.

"Reyna and I swapped," Simon said, "on account of the beers I'd already drunk." A wicked smile. Simon had always been able to get away with anything, he was too funny, too quick with it. You couldn't stay mad at him. Well, Maddy could, if she was really trying.

"Hey, Reyna's really cool, by the way," Simon whispered to Maddy, as though she had some claim over the coolness of her brother's girlfriend. But she smiled and took it anyway, a glance over at the couple, picture-perfect, even with their backs turned.

A break in the conversation; now was the time to ask before Red forgot.

"Hey, Maddy, about the sofa bed—"

"—Shit!" Oliver hissed up front, an ugly sound. "This is our exit right here. Move over, Reyna. Now! NOW."

"I can't," Reyna said, suddenly flustered, checking her mirrors and flipping the turn signal.

"They'll move for you, we're bigger, just go," Oliver said, reaching forward like he might grab the wheel himself.

A screeching sound, not from the RV but from Reyna, as she pulled the hulking vehicle across one lane. An angry Chevrolet screamed on its horn, and the guy at the wheel threw up a middle finger, holding it out the window. Red pretended to catch it, slipping it into the chest pocket of her blue-and-yellow-check shirt, treasuring it forever.

"Move, move, move," Oliver barked, and Reyna swerved right again, making the exit just in time. Another horn, this time from a furious Tesla they left behind on the highway.

"We could have just come off at the next one and worked it out. That's what Google Maps is for," Reyna said, slowing down, her voice strange and squished like it was working its way through gritted teeth. Red had never seen Reyna flustered before, or angry, only ever smiling, wider each time she checked in with Oliver's eyes. What was that like, to be in love? She couldn't imagine it; that was why she watched them sometimes, learning by example. But Red should have said something about the exit earlier, shouldn't she? They'd made it almost all day without any raised voices. That was her fault.

"I'm sorry," Oliver said now, tucking Reyna's thick black hair behind her ear so he could squeeze her shoulder, imprinting his fingers. "I just want to get to the campsite ASAP. We're all tired."

Red looked away, leaving them alone in their moment, well, as alone as they could get in an RV with six people, thirty-one feet long. Apparently that extra foot was so important they couldn't round it down.

The world on her side of the RV was dark again. Trees lined the road, but Red could hardly see them, not past her own reflection and the other face hiding beneath it. She had to look away from that too, before she thought about it too much. Not here, not now.

The truck in front slowed as it passed a SPEED LIMIT 35 sign, its brake lights staining the road red ahead of them. The color that followed her wherever she went, and it never meant anything good. But the road moved on, and so did they.

Oh wait, what was it she needed to ask Maddy about again?

TWO

A strange yawning in Red's gut, the sound hidden by the wheels on the road. She couldn't be hungry, could she? They'd only stopped for dinner at a rest stop a few hours ago. But the feeling doubled down, twisting again, so she reached out for the bag of chips in front of Maddy. She removed a handful, placing them carefully in her mouth one by one, cheese dust coating her fingertips.

"Oh yeah," Simon said, standing up and sidling out of the booth, heading toward his bunk beyond the mini-kitchen. "And youse all owe me seven bucks for the snacks I got at the gas station."

Red stared down at the chips left in her hand.

"Hey." Maddy leaned over the table. "I'll cover you for the snacks, don't worry about it."

Red swallowed. Looked down even farther to hide her eyes from Maddy. Not worrying wasn't a choice, not one Red had anyway. In her darkest moments, those winter nights when she had to wear her coat to bed, over two pairs of pajamas and five pairs of socks, and still shivered anyway, Red sometimes wished she were Maddy Lavoy. To live in that warm house as though it belonged to her, to have everything they had and everything she didn't anymore.

Stop that. She felt a flush in her cheeks. Shame was a red feeling, a hot one, just like guilt and anger. Why couldn't the Kennys heat their home on guilt and shame alone? But things would get better soon, right? Real soon, that was the plan, what it was all for. And then everything would be different. How freeing it would be to just do or think, and not have to double-think or triple-think, or say *No thank you, maybe next time.* To not beg for extra shifts at work and lose sleep either way. To take another handful of chips just because she wanted to.

Red realized she hadn't said anything yet. "Thanks," she mumbled, keeping her eyes to herself, but she didn't take any more chips, it didn't feel right. She'd just have to live with that feeling in her gut. And maybe it wasn't hunger after all that.

"No worries," Maddy said. There, see, she didn't have any. Maddy had no need for worries. She was one of those people who was good at everything, first try. Well, apart from that time she insisted on taking up the harp. Unless Red was one of Maddy's worries. It did seem that way sometimes.

"Are we in South Carolina yet?" Red said, changing the subject, one thing *she* was good at.

"Not yet," Oliver called behind, though he wasn't the Lavoy she'd asked. "Soon. I think we should be at the campsite in around forty minutes."

"Woohoo, spring break!" Simon yelled again in a high-pitched voice, and somehow he had another bottle of beer in his hand, the refrigerator door swinging open behind him.

"I got it," Arthur said, passing an unsteady Simon in the narrow space between the sofa bed and the dining table, clapping him on the back. Arthur darted forward to catch the refrigerator door and pushed it shut, the dim overhead lights flashing against his gold-framed glasses as he turned. Red liked his glasses, standing out against his tan skin and curly dark brown hair. She wondered whether she needed glasses; faraway things seem to have gotten farther and fuzzier lately. Another thing to add to the to-worry list, because she couldn't do anything about it. Yet. Arthur caught her looking, smiling as he ran a finger over the light stubble on his chin.

"Given up on Twenty Questions, have you?" he asked them both.

"Red forgot her person, place or thing," Maddy said, and that made Red think: Wasn't there something else she'd forgotten, something she wanted to ask Maddy?

"Chip?" Maddy offered the bag to Arthur.

"Ah, I'm good, thanks." He backed away from the bag, almost tripping over the corner of the sofa bed. A look clouded his eyes, and now that she was looking, was there a slight sheen of sweat on his forehead? Red didn't normally catch these things, but this one she did. Did that mean she looked at him too often?

"What's up?" she said. "Deathly allergic to cheese puffs?"

"No, thankfully," Arthur said, feeling his way as he sat down on the sofa bed.

Oh yes, Red needed to ask Maddy about which side she slept on. Shit, Arthur had just said something and she hadn't listened. Best to go with a well-placed "Huh?"

"I said at least I don't feel as dizzy as Simon probably does."

"Carsick?" Red said. "Well, RV-sick?"

"No, it's not that." Arthur shook his head. "Probably far too late to be telling you all this, but I'm not that great with tight spaces." He looked around at the crammed-in furniture and the compact kitchen. "I thought it would be wider—"

"That's what she said!" Simon interrupted.

"For god's sake, Simon, enough with *The Office* references," Maddy said. "He's been doing that since middle school, before he even knew what it meant."

"I'm standing right here, Mads, don't third-person me."

"Can you all shut up for a second?" Oliver spoke over Maddy's retort. "We're trying to navigate over here."

Red turned back to Arthur. "Well, good thing you're not spending a whole week in this cramped RV. Oh . . . wait." Red smiled at him.

"I know, right."

Arthur was Simon's friend, really, but he was all of theirs by now. He didn't go to their high school, he went to one in South Philly, but he and Simon were on the same basketball team, both joined last year sometime. Red guessed Arthur didn't much like his friends at his own school, because he'd been coming to all their parties and hangouts since senior year began. And that was okay, because she liked having him around. He always asked how she was and how was her day, even though Red usually answered with lies or exaggerated stories with only faint traces of the truth. He showed interest when Red wasn't interesting at all. And there was that time he dropped her home after that New Year's Eve party and let her sit in his car, warming up in the dry air of the heater before she had to go inside the cold house and find whatever mess her dad had left for her. Arthur didn't know that was happening, he thought they were just talking, talking the night away at two in the morning outside her house. A small kindness he never knew he'd given her. She should give him one back.

"We'll be at the campsite soon, I think," she said. "You can get out and stretch your legs in the great big outdoors. I'll come with you."

"Yeah." Arthur smiled. "I'll be fine." His gaze dropped from her face to the table, where she was resting one hand. "I was meaning to ask earlier, but I didn't want to distract you from driving. What does your hand say?"

"Oh." Red blushed, raising the hand and rubbing at it self-consciously, realizing as she did that there was something written on the back of that one too. To-do lists everywhere, even on her own body. To-do lists and never-get-done lists. "I've got a two-for-one special for you," she said. "On our left hand, we have: *Call AT&T*."

"Ah, I see. Fascinating. What about?" he asked.

"You know," Red said. "Just to check in with them, see how they're doing, whether they had a good day."

Arthur nodded, a wry smile to match hers. "And did you do it?"

Red pursed her lips, looking at the empty box she'd drawn near her knuckle. "No," she said. "I ran out of time."

"And hand number two?"

"On hand number two," Red said, drawing out the suspense, "we have the very elaborate and detailed instruction: *Pack*."

"You must have done that one," Arthur said.

"Just about," she replied like it was a joke, but she was telling the truth this time. Packed literally right before she left the house this morning, no time to even double-check her bag against her list. She'd been too busy making sure there was enough food in the house for her dad while she was away.

"Well, if you did it, why haven't you checked it off?" Arthur said, pointing to the small empty box on the see-through flesh of her hand. "Here." He stood up, grabbing one of Maddy's pens from the table that she'd used in an earlier game of Hangman. He uncapped it and leaned toward Red, pressing the felt-tip end against her skin. Gently, he drew two lines: a check mark in the little box. "There you go," he said, standing back to admire his handiwork.

Red looked at her hand. And it felt stupid to admit it to herself, but the sight of that little check mark did change something in her. Small, minuscule, a tiny firework bursting in her head, but it felt good. It always felt good, checking off those boxes. She held out her hand proudly for Maddy to examine and got the nod of approval she was looking for.

Arthur was still watching her, a look in his eyes, a different one that Red couldn't decipher.

"Brazil nuts," Red said.

Arthur's face screwed up. "What?"

"I used to be allergic to them as a kid, but I'm not anymore. Isn't that weird, that a person can just change like that?" she said, fidgeting with the front pocket of her light blue jeans. She'd been sitting here in this spot a long time now. Too long. "My mo—p-parents had to write it on my hand, so I wouldn't forget. Also, does the pattern in the curtains remind anyone of something?" She touched the white-and-blue curtain hanging down next to her, running her hand between the pleats. "It's been bugging me all day, can't work out what it is. A cartoon or something."

"It's just a random pattern," Maddy answered.

"No, it's something. It's something." Red traced her finger over it. Like the silhouette of a character she couldn't quite place. From a book she was read at night, or a TV show? Either way, best not to think back to that time, to when she was little, because of who else might be there.

"Tomatoes," Arthur said, saving her from the memory. "Give me a rash around my mouth. Only when raw, though." He straightened up, as did the wrinkles in his white baseball jersey, navy on the arms. "Anyway, I think I better help with the directions. I'm sensing that Simon is being a hindrance."

"I'm doing a stellar job, thank you very much," Simon said, looking over Oliver's shoulder at an iPhone with a marble orange case; must be Reyna's. There was a map on the screen, a blue dot moving along a highlighted road. The blue dot was them, the six of them and all thirty-one feet of RV. Thank god it wasn't a red dot. Blue was safer.

Arthur sidled to the front, blocking Red's view of the screen, her eyes falling instead to Maddy, who gave her a not-so-subtle wink.

"Huh?"

Maddy shushed her silently, nodding her head ever so slightly in Arthur's direction. "Checks all the boxes," she whispered.

"Stop it," Red warned her.

"You stop it."

They both stopped, because just then Maddy's phone rang, an angry-wasp buzz against the table. The screen lit up with the view from the front camera: the off-white ceiling and a sliver of the under-side of Maddy's chin. Across the top was the word *Mom* and *FaceTime video*, with a *slide to answer* button waiting patiently at the bottom.

Maddy's reaction was instant. Too quick. She tensed, bones sharpening beneath her skin. Her hand darted out to grab the phone, holding it up and away to hide it from Red.

Red knew that was what she was doing, she always knew, though Maddy didn't know she knew.

"I'll call her when we get to the campsite," Maddy said, almost too quiet to hear over the wheels, pressing the side button to reject the call. Looking anywhere but at Red.

Mom.

Like Maddy thought Red would split open and bleed just to see the word.

It had been the same for years. In freshman year, Maddy used to take kids to the side and tell them off for saying *yo Momma* jokes in front of Red. She didn't think Red would ever find out. It was a forbidden word, a dirty word. She even got weird talking about the Mummers Parade in front of Red.

How ridiculous.

Except, the thing was, Maddy wasn't wrong.

Red did bleed just to see the word, to hear it, to think it, to remember, the guilt leaving a crater in her chest. Blood, red as her name and red as her shame. So, she didn't think it, or remember, and she wouldn't look to the left to see her mom's face in her reflection in the window. No, she wouldn't. These eyes were just hers.

THREE

Red concentrated on staring ahead. She wanted to think about the pattern in the curtains again, but she couldn't risk looking that way. Instead, she looked down at the check mark drawn on her hand, eyes tracing the lines, trying to summon back that tiny firework.

Maddy placed her phone facedown.

"Shall we play another game?" she said.

If Red had to sit here any longer, she might go mad. Even just walking a few laps of the RV might help. Thirty-one feet, you know, not just thirty. The 2017 GetAway Vista 31B. 2017 was also the year that—no, stop.

She was about to stand up when the sound of a duck quacking stopped her, mechanical and insistent. It was coming from behind her head.

"Oh, that's me," Oliver said, jumping up from the passenger seat and squeezing his wide shoulders past Arthur and Simon. "Mom's calling," he said.

Red breathed in.

"How do you know it's your mom without looking?" Simon asked, a look of genuine confusion on his face.

"Personalized ringtone," Oliver said, walking past the dining table to the tiny kitchen, running his hands through his golden-brown hair, the exact same shade as his eyes. His backpack was sitting on the counter. He unzipped it. "My mom started it; has personalized ringtones for the whole family," he explained, digging his hand inside. "She has duck à l'orange for her birthday meal every year. Hence the duck." He found the ringing phone, pulled it out. "Arthur, can you take over directions?"

"No problem." Arthur took the empty seat.

"Hey, Mom," Oliver said, holding the phone out to get a good view of his face. He stepped forward and slid onto the booth beside Red. Catherine Lavoy's face filled the screen, her hair the same color as Oliver's, neat and curled. Faint lines around her eyes as she smiled out of the phone. She looked tired, her face full of shadows.

"Hello, sweetie," she said, an uncharacteristic croakiness catching her voice. She cleared her throat. "I just tried Madeline but she wasn't picking up."

"I'm here, Mom," Maddy said, with an awkward glance at Red, but Red pretended not to notice. It was stupid anyway because Red liked Catherine. More than liked her. Catherine had been there Red's entire life. She was kind and caring, and she always knew just how to help her. And, most importantly, she always cut sandwiches into triangles. Oliver pressed the button to activate the rear camera so Maddy could wave at her mom. "Sorry, I didn't hear it ringing."

"That's okay," Catherine said. "Just calling to check how you guys are doing. Are you at your stopover point yet?"

Oliver pressed the front camera on again, and Red could see from the direction of his gaze that he was looking into his own face, shifting his angles so the light found his cheekbones. "No, not yet, we're close to the campsite I think, though. Hey, where are we?" he called to those at the front.

Arthur checked over his shoulder. "Driving through a *Morven Township*. Should be around twenty-five minutes."

"Who was that?" Catherine asked, searching the corners of her screen as though they could give her the answer.

"Maddy's friend, Arthur," Oliver said.

"Who's driving?" Catherine asked.

"Reyna is currently."

"Hi, Mrs. Lavoy," Reyna called from the front, not taking her eyes off the dark road.

"Hello, Reyna," Catherine shouted back, too loudly, her voice crackling against the speakers. "Okay, so you're almost there?"

"Correct."

"Great. Oh, is that Red there?" Catherine asked, peering into her screen, raising it closer to her eye.

Oliver tilted the phone, trapping Red inside the camera. She smiled.

"Oh, it is! Hello, sweetie, how's it going?"

"Yeah, good. No official complaints to file."

Catherine laughed. "And are my children behaving? You know I trust you the—"

Catherine froze on the screen, dead pixels distorting her face.

"The—"

Her hand jolted across the screen, blending into the mess of her face. No longer a person, just blocks of muted color.

"Mom?" Oliver said.

"Th . . . th . . ."

Her words scattered into layers, robotic and strange.

Red's image was frozen too, eyes wide, afraid she'd be stuck in Oliver's phone forever.

"Mom, can you hear me?" Oliver said. "Mom?"

"Ca . . . n you g . . . uys hear me? Hello?" Catherine's voice broke through, but her face couldn't keep up, mouthing words that already existed, talking before she could speak.

"Got you," Oliver said. "Well, sort of. Guess the service must be spotty around here."

"Okay, well." Catherine's face fast-forwarded, twitching as it dragged itself to the present. "I'll let you get on with . . . is that a beer bottle?" Catherine's eye moved to the camera again, staring at a shape on the counter behind Oliver's shoulder.

"Yeah, it's mine," Oliver said smoothly, without a beat. He might just be a better liar than Red.

"You aren't drinking on this trip, are you, Maddy?" Catherine raised her voice to find her daughter off-screen.

"No, Mom," Maddy began. "I know—"

"—You are seventeen, I don't want to hear from anyone that you've been drinking. You can have fun without it."

Which reminded Red; Maddy turned eighteen in just a couple of weeks. She was already worrying about how to get her a birthday present.

"Yes, I know. I am. I won't," Maddy said, leaning forward so her mom could hear her more clearly.

"Oliver?"

"Yes, Mom. I'll watch her. Take chaperone duties very seriously, won't we, Reyna?"

"Yes ma'am," Reyna called.

"All right." Catherine eased back from the camera. "I'll let you go, then. I've got some prep to get on with. Text me in the morning before you head off again."

"Will do, Mom," Oliver said.

"Okay, bye everyone, bye Red."

They called "Bye" in clashing tones, Simon going high and shrill for some reason.

"Love you, Oliver, Maddy."

"Love you, Mom," they said in perfect Lavoy synchronization, and Oliver thumbed the red button, disappearing Catherine back to that warm house in Philadelphia.

"Whew." Maddy breathed out. "What more does she want? My big brother and his girlfriend are already accompanying me on spring break at her insistence. It's so annoying."

She was talking to Red, she must have been, because just then her eyes flashed and she snatched them away, realizing she'd been complaining to the one with the dead mom. But that was okay because Red was thinking about the cartoon *Phineas and Ferb;* they weren't a match for the pattern in the curtains, but now the full theme song was running through her head.

"It's fine," Oliver said to his sister. "Reyna and I are renting our own condo. You won't even see us; we'll leave you and all your friends to it. Wouldn't catch me staying in an RV for a whole week with a bunch of teenagers."

"Yeah," Maddy said, directing her voice at her brother now, "but Mom doesn't know about that part."

"And what Mom doesn't know can't hurt her. She's just stressed with work stuff at the moment," Oliver said, coming to his mom's defense. He did that a lot.

Red really wanted to stand up now, to escape this conversation, to go stand with Arthur at the front, but Oliver and his wide shoulders were trapping her here. Simon came and sat down too, just to make the situation worse, dropping in beside Maddy and digging his hand through the bag of chips. He shoveled an entire fistful into his mouth.

"Yeah, I know," Maddy said, cheeks still flushed. "But she doesn't have to take it out on me."

"She's just protective of you," Oliver countered.

"What are youse all talking about?" Simon said, spewing orange crumbs from his mouth as he did.

"My mom," Oliver explained. "She's stressed because she's in the middle of this huge case at the moment."

"Oh yeah, she's a lawyer, right?" Simon asked, going in for more chips.

Oliver did not look amused. "She's assistant district attorney," he said, and it was hard to miss the pride in his voice, the way he over-pronounced those three words. Which Red translated to mean: *No, Simon, you idiot, she's not* just *a lawyer.*

"What's the case?" Simon said, oblivious to the disdain on Oliver's face.

"You've probably heard about it on the news," he said, pointedly. "It's a pretty big deal."

A huge deal, Red thought.

"It's a homicide case; a murder involving two members of the biggest organized crime gang in the city," Oliver said, a shadow of disappointment in his eyes as he didn't get the reaction he was looking for from Simon. He elaborated: "The *literal* Philadelphia Mafia."

"Oh, cool," Simon said, between bites. "Didn't know the Mafia was still a thing, I love *The Godfather.* 'Revenge is a dish best served cold,' " he said in a dreadful Italian American accent.

"Very much still a thing," Oliver said, settling in to his story now that he had Simon's attention.

Could Red climb under the table to get out? Urgh, no: too many legs.

"There was some leadership dispute going on in the crime family, I won't bore you with the details. And at the end of August last year, one of the leaders, Joseph Mannino, was killed by another, Francesco Gotti. Allegedly, I should say. Shot him twice in the back of the head."

Red tried not to picture it, studying the curtains again. She had heard it all so many times; she probably knew the details even better than Oliver. Not that she was going to say so.

"We are officially in South Carolina!" Arthur called, pointing to a green sign out the front, illuminated by the RV's headlights.

Oliver kept talking: "Mom is the lead prosecutor taking Frank Gotti to trial for the murder. The pretrial conference is in a couple of weeks—"

April 25 to be exact, Red thought, surprised she had remembered that particular detail. That wasn't like her.

"—and then it's jury selection and the actual trial."

"Cool," Simon said again. "Mrs. Lavoy, taking on the mob."

Oliver seemed to swell a little, sitting up taller, blocking Red in even more. "But it's not just all that. She had to fight to even get this case. Normally a crime like this would be considered a federal case and would be tried by the US attorney's office. They've tried to prosecute Frank Gotti multiple times, on various charges like drug trafficking and racketeering, and have never once got a conviction. But Mom managed to argue that this murder was under the DA's jurisdiction because it wasn't specifically related to drug trafficking and because Frank Gotti killed Mannino himself; he didn't pay a hit man like they normally do."

Simon yawned; Oliver was losing his crowd. But he didn't take the hint.

"And we know that," Oliver continued, "because there was an eyewitness. Someone actually saw Frank Gotti walking away after shooting Mannino dead. And that's why Mom's so stressed—because the entire case rests on this witness's testimony. And, as you can imagine, in cases against the Mafia, lead witnesses are often intimidated out of testifying or straight-up killed. So Mom has had to make sure the witness has been kept entirely anonymous in all the court documents. *Witness A* is what the press are calling him."

"I see," Simon said. Did he regret asking? Red certainly regretted having to hear it all again.

"But if she wins this case," Oliver said, eyes flashing as though this were the most important part of the story, so Simon better stay with him, "it will be career-defining. The current DA is retiring after this term, and if Mom gets this conviction, she's basically guaranteed to win the Democratic primary this year and be elected DA."

"Let's not jinx it," Maddy chimed in, and it was nice to hear someone else's voice for a change, other than Oliver's and the one in Red's head.

"No"—Oliver nodded down at his sister—"but I'm saying, if Frank Gotti is found guilty, Mom has a great chance of becoming DA." He turned back to Simon. Poor Simon. "Her biggest competition at the moment is Mo Frazer, another assistant DA. He's very popular, especially with the African American communities, but if Mom gets this conviction, I think it will give her the edge over him."

Oliver finally drew back, bowing his head like he was waiting for someone to personally congratulate him.

"Congratulations," Red said, resisting the urge to add one small clap. Simon took the opportunity to escape.

"Shut up, Red," Oliver replied, trying to make it a joke. There were times when Red thought of Oliver as a borrowed big brother; she'd known him her entire life, longer than Maddy if you thought about it like that. But then there were other times she wasn't even sure he remembered her name. Not like it was a difficult one: think primary colors.

"She's done incredibly well for herself. DA before the age of fifty. Of course, by that time I'm going to be US attorney general," he said, again like it was a joke, but it really really wasn't. Oliver managed to turn everything into a dick-measuring contest. Red snorted at that, giving the voice in her head a pat on the back.

"What?" Oliver turned to her, his wide shoulders even wider now, a blockade either side of his neck. "Okay, so what are you doing with your life? I actually can't remember which college you're going to this year, remind me?"

A lump in Red's throat.

"Harvard," she said without blinking. "Full-ride scholarship."

Oliver's eyes snapped wider, bottom lip hanging open. She had just one-upped his prelaw at Dartmouth with a premed girlfriend, how dare she? Red enjoyed the look while she could.

"Wh . . . R-really?" he said.

"Yeah," she said. "Early admission."

"Red," Maddy said in a mock-warning voice, her eyes silently scolding. She used to enjoy annoying Oliver too.

"What?" Oliver looked between them.

"I'm not going to college this year," Red said, relenting. It was fun while it lasted, living that other life.

Oliver laughed, a sigh of relief buried in there somewhere. "I was going to say. Full scholarship at Harvard, ha! Didn't think so."

Oh he didn't, did he?

"You're not going anywhere?" he asked now, fully recovered from the shock.

"Red missed the application deadline," Maddy explained for her. Which wasn't the truth, but it was a good lie, a convenient one, because how very *Red* it was.

"You know me," Red said, just to hammer it home.

"How could you miss the deadline?" Oliver turned to her, a look of cold concern on his face, and Red didn't like where this was going, but she was trapped right here in this fucking booth forever.

She shrugged, hoping that would shut him down.

It did not, Oliver opening his mouth to speak again.

"I don't understand it," he said. "You were such a smart kid."

Don't say it, please don't say it.

"Seems a shame," Oliver went on. "You had so much potential."

And there it was. The line that ripped her open. She'd lost count of the number of times it had been said to her, but there was only one that truly mattered. Red was thirteen and Mom was alive, screaming at each other across the kitchen, back when it used to be warm.

"Red?" Maddy was saying.

It was too hot in here.

Red stood up, knocking her knees against the table, swaying as the RV turned.

"I gotta go—"

But she was saved by Arthur, calling: "Shit, I think we went the wrong way."

FOUR

"What do you mean?"

Oliver got up from the booth—thank God, Red was free—and walked the four strides to the front, nudging Simon out of his way.

"Let me see," he said to Arthur, holding his hand out for the phone with the directions.

Red was free and she wasn't about to sit at this table any longer. She sidled along and out, moving toward the congregation at the front, perching on the corner of the sofa bed. Oh yes, now she remembered.

"Maddy, which side—"

"—No, it's fine." Oliver spoke across her, swiping his finger on the screen. "It's redirected us. Just keep going down this road, it takes us past a small town called Ruby. Then it should be a left turn and we go south for a bit, toward the *Carolina Sandhills National Wildlife Refuge,*" he read from the screen. "Campsite is right around there. We should be just over ten minutes, everyone."

"Perfect," Reyna said, taking one hand off the wheel to rub at her eyes.

"You getting tired?" Oliver asked her. "I can take over?" His voice was different when he spoke to Reyna. Softer at the edges.

"No, I'm good," she said, shooting him a quick smile over her shoulder, stretching wide across her light brown skin. It seemed almost a waste, that a smile that nice was meant for Oliver. That was a mean thought. He meant well. Everyone always meant well.

"You okay?" Arthur asked Red, vacating the passenger seat so Oliver could take it and coming to stand beside her.

She nodded. "RV feels smaller when you've been in it for ten-plus hours."

"I hear that," he agreed. "We'll be there soon. Or we could both get shit-faced like Simon and we won't care anymore."

"I'm not shit-faced," Simon said from behind Arthur. "I'm a very comfortable-amount drunk."

"I'm not so sure Tomorrow Morning Simon will agree," Red said.

"I'm not sure Now Maddy agrees either," Maddy said, turning around and perching on her booth so she could see them all. "You don't want to peak too soon. We have a whole week ahead of us."

Simon finished off his beer in one large gulp, eyeballing Maddy as he did so.

"Is it this left turn here?" Reyna asked, slowing down. "Oliver?"

"Sorry, um . . ." He stared down at the phone in his hands. "The GPS has gone weird. I think I've lost service. I'm not sure where we are."

"I need an answer," Reyna said, idling to a stop just ahead of the intersection, hand hesitating over the turn signal.

A car horn sounded behind them. And again.

"Oliver?" Reyna said, her voice rising, the knuckles bursting out of her skin like bony hilltops as she held the wheel too hard.

"Um, yes, I think so. Left here," he said, uncertainly.

But it was all Reyna needed; she pushed off and took the turn, the car behind screaming its displeasure as it zipped off across the intersection.

"Asshole," she said under her breath.

"Sorry," Oliver said. "Your phone isn't working."

"Not you, the car," Reyna clarified.

"I can't get the map to work," Oliver said, swiping furiously at the screen, closing the map app and reopening it. It was blank; a yellow background and empty grid lines and nothing else. "It doesn't know where we are. Zero bars. Hey, does anyone have any service?"

Red had left her phone over there on the table. But if she had zero bars, it could mean she had no signal, or it could mean that AT&T finally cut off her service after the last unpaid bill.

"I've got a bar," Arthur said, his phone cupped in his hand.

"Who's your provider?" Oliver looked up at him.

"Verizon," he said. "Hold on, I'll get the route up." He tapped at his screen. "Already had it loaded from when I was directing Red. Okay, so yeah we took the correct turn. You keep on this road for two miles, then it's a right down Bo Melton Loop."

"My phone is struggling too," Maddy said, holding it up and shaking it, like that might spark some life back into it.

"We're deep in the country now, folks," Simon said, leaning on his words in an atrocious Southern accent, spliced with a touch of *crazy old man*. Sober Simon was normally quite good at accents. He prided himself on them, in fact, always guaranteed a part in the school play. You should hear his upper-class English gentleman.

Red watched out the wide windshield, a panoramic view of darkness, the two headlights carving up the night, bringing it into existence. There was no world anymore, only this RV and the six of them, and whatever the dark brought them.

Arthur made a small noise: a groan in the back of his throat as he stared down at his screen. Red stood up, looking over his shoulder to see what it was. He glanced back at her and cleared his throat. Maybe she was standing too close.

"Looks like I just lost service too," he said, right as Red's eyes registered the zero bars at the top of the screen.

"Shit," Oliver hissed, tapping Reyna's phone again, like he could make it work through sheer force of will. If anyone could, a Lavoy could.

"It's okay," Arthur said to him, "I still have the route up, just can't see where we are on it. We'll have to look for road signs."

"Old-school navigation," Reyna commented.

"Let me help," Simon said, shuffling over to Arthur and Red, crowding them. "I'm good at maps."

"You say you're good at everything," Red said.

"I *am* good at everything," Simon answered. "Except being humble."

There was no one else on the road. No passing headlights, no red glow of brake lights up ahead. Red stared out the windshield, concentrated.

"When's the turn?" Reyna asked.

"Not yet," Red answered, her eyes now following the highlighted road on Arthur's screen, no blue dot to guide them, trying to match it with the darkness outside.

"Wouldn't trust Red with directions," Maddy said.

"Hey."

"Well, I mean, it's not like you're ever on time, is it?"

Red leaned back to look at Maddy perching on the booth, head resting on the bed of her knuckles. "I'll have you know," she said, "that everyone else was later than me this morning. I was first by like ten whole minutes."

Maddy looked sheepish, biting one lip.

"What?"

"Nothing."

Red knew it wasn't nothing.

"Maddy, what?"

"I, um, I told you we were meeting at our house at nine. But I told everyone else we were meeting at ten."

"You told me a whole hour earlier?" Red said, and why did it sting that she had? It was a lie, yes, but it was a considerate lie. Maddy knew Red would be late: she didn't know all the reasons why, but she knew the end result and that was the same, wasn't it?

"So technically, you were fifty minutes late and everyone else was on time."

"I missed the bus," Red said, which wasn't true: she spent the last of her change on her dad's favorite cereal and then walked the whole way, bag wheeling behind her.

"Ha, look, that road's called Wagon Wheel Road," Simon snorted, pointing at the screen.

"Is that the right I make?" Reyna asked, hand darting to the turn signal, though there was no one to signal for.

No, it wasn't here.

"No, no, no," Arthur said quickly. "It's the next one. I think."

Reyna sped up again, following the road as it curved around.

"Wagon Wheel." Simon was still chuckling to himself.

"Here, this right," Oliver said, taking charge. "Turn, Reyna."

"I'm turning," she said, the faintest trace of irritation in her voice. Too many cooks. Which made Reyna, what? A spoon? The Lavoys had fancy spoons at their house: pearly handles and no stains.

There was a new sound, joining with the wind as it rushed against the sides of the RV: a rasping noise beneath them. The road was growing rougher, gravelly, the RV lurching as it rolled down. There were no more yellow markings, no more *my lane* and *your lane,* and from the light of the high beams Red could see rows and rows of trees standing either side, silent sentinels on the dead-of-night road.

She felt watched, which was stupid; trees didn't have eyes. But neither did doors, yet her mom used to stick googly ones on Red's so she felt safe in her bed in the dar— No, stop, she needed to concentrate on where they were going.

"Looks like we're in the middle of nowhere," Maddy commented from her perch, cupping her hands around her eyes so she could look out the side window.

"As is the campsite, so we're good," Oliver replied.

The RV staggered as it hit a pothole.

Arthur was chewing his lip, eyes narrowed behind his glasses. "I think it's left here," he said, not sure, not loud enough to reach Reyna.

"Left, left here!" Simon didn't have the same problem. But Reyna didn't listen, didn't trust the drunk one.

"It's left," Red said.

"You sure?" Oliver asked her, but Reyna had already pulled the RV into it, and the road wasn't even paved anymore, just dirt and rocks, dust kicking up into the headlights. "This can't be right, let me look at the map." He snapped his fingers for Arthur to pass his phone over. "Reyna, turn around."

"I can't turn around!" she said, more than a hint of irritation in her voice now: a full underlayer. "This road is way too narrow and this RV is way too big."

"Where are we?" Red asked Arthur, leaning across to see, like it made any difference.

"I think we're here somewhere." He pointed at the screen. "McNair Cemetery Road. Maybe."

"That's definitely wrong," Oliver said. "We have to turn ba—"

"—I can't!" Reyna shot him a look.

"Is there a turn?" Red nudged Arthur.

"Wait, I think there's a left soon," he said, zooming in to the mouth of the small road on his phone. "Might circle us back to that other road." He glanced at Red and she nodded.

"For fuck's sake," Oliver said, one of his knees rattling against the dashboard. "We wouldn't have gone the wrong way if I was directing."

"This is stressful," Maddy said, her hands buried in her loose hair. "We should have just flown and rented a condo like everyone else from school is."

A flush in Maddy's cheeks as she realized what she'd said, their eyes meeting for half a second. Red was the reason they didn't fly and rent a condo like everyone else. That was why Maddy came up with the RV idea. *Way cheaper—just gas and spending money. Come on, it will be fun.* It was all Red's fault.

"Just keep going," Red said to Reyna, blocking everyone else out.

"I don't see a left turn." Reyna leaned closer to the wheel, straining to see.

As they followed the corner around, the headlights got lost in the woods, recoiling as they bounded off some body of water: a creek hiding somewhere behind the trees.

"Where's the left turn?" Reyna pushed forward.

"There!" Simon pointed out the windshield. "It's here. Go left."

"Sure?"

Red glanced down at the map in Arthur's hands. This was it. "Yes," she said. "Down there."

"Doesn't even look like a real road," Oliver said as they peeled down it, dirt and gravel loud against the wheels.

It was narrower, tighter, the trees pressing in on them, barring the way with low-hanging branches that scraped the top of the RV.

"Keep going," Red said. Her fault that the others were here and not on a nice plane tomorrow instead, with all their other friends.

"I've lost the map," Arthur said, blank grid lines taking over his screen.

"Keep going," she said.

"Not like we have a choice," Oliver retorted.

The trees broke away from the road, cutting their losses, giving way to low-lying scrubland and long grass on either side.

"Is it a dead end?" Oliver asked, staring out the front.

"Keep going," Red said.

"Pretty sure it's a dead end," Oliver decided, though none of them could see. "Reyna, it's wide enough here, you can turn around and head back."

"Okay." Reyna gave in, pushing her foot against the brake.

The RV slowed, rattling against the barely-there road.

A sharper sound, like a crack, splitting the night in half.

"What was that?" Simon asked.

The RV hitched, drooping down at the front left side, Red stumbling into Arthur as it did.

"Fuck," Oliver said, staring at Reyna over there on the sunken side, slamming his fist into the dashboard. "I think we just punctured a tire."